Make You Mine This Christmas

Rachel Holm

Ebook ISBN: (9798986576282)
Paperback ISBN: 9781969654008
https://www.rachelwholm.com/
Cover Design: Brooke-Gilbert
Editor: On the Page Editorial
Proofreader: Weaver Way Author Services

 Formatted with Vellum

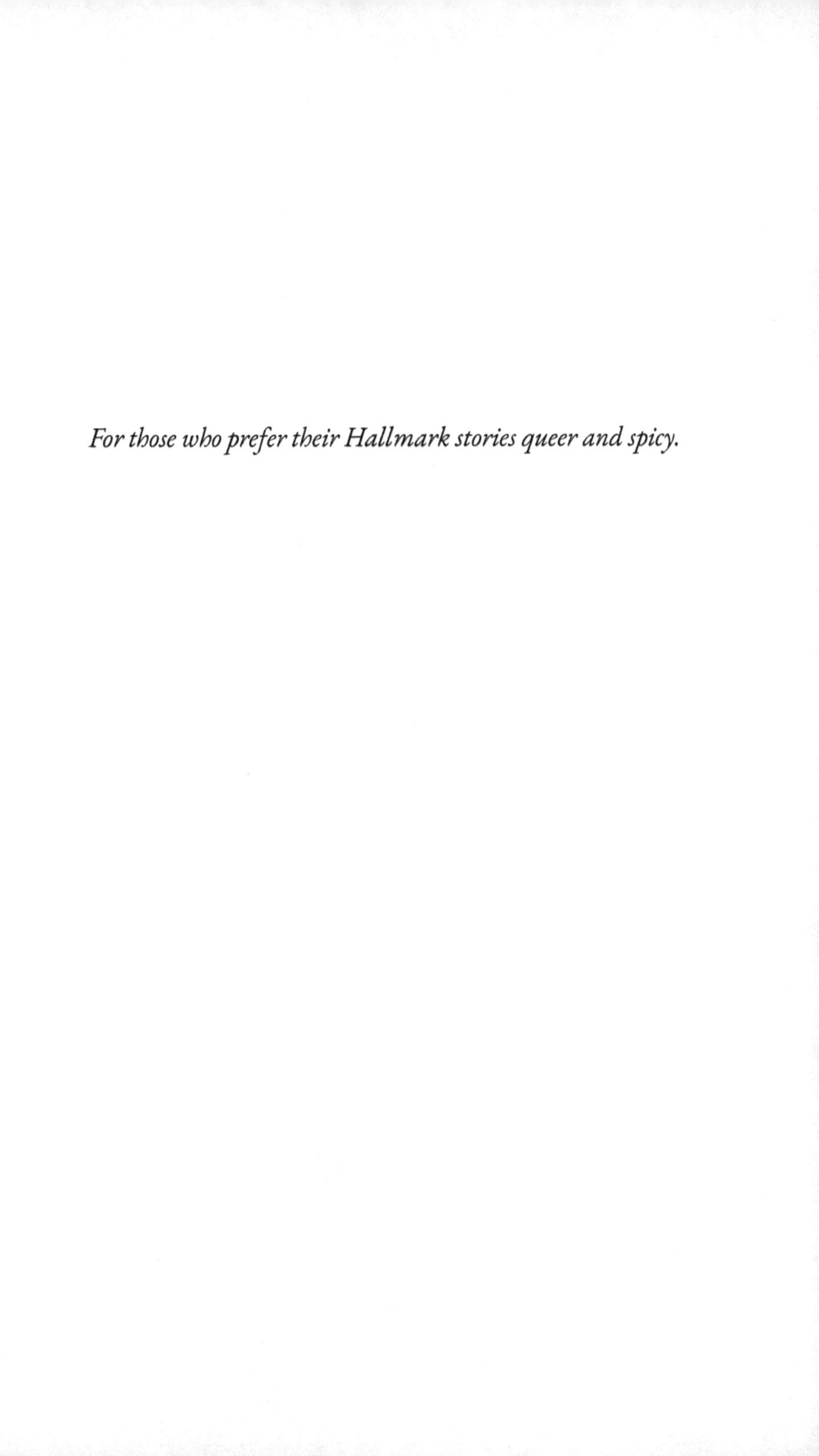

For those who prefer their Hallmark stories queer and spicy.

A Note From the Author

Welcome (back) to Holly Ridge!

When I set out to write Carry Me Through Christmas, I never imagined it would be the spark for the shared Rachel-verse I write in today. Blaire and Cole's best friends stole the show in that one, and I'm so happy to finally get the fourth member of their group his Happy Ever After. Being back in this happy little New England town I dreamt up all those years ago (2020 to be exact) felt like coming home.

As a second chance romance, this story trends a bit angstier than my previous books, but you'll still find the same funny and lighthearted moments around that angst you've come to expect from my books. It is also probably my spiciest yet. (Sorry Dad)

As always, I like to include some content notes for anyone who feels they may benefit from them. I've made my best efforts to handle any representation or situation depicted in this book with respect and care; any failure to do so lies with me alone.

Content Notes: Strained Parental Relationship (past), mention of panic attacks (past) ; Limited mentions of caretaking for parent with Cancer (past), mentions of current scans (Character on page with No Evidence of Disease (NED)); Contains adult language and explicit, open-door intimate scenes.

Chapter 1

Austin

"Please, Austin, we're one elf short." My best friend Cole sounds exhausted and I can one of the twins—or both—crying in the background. "Blaire would have called you herself, but she ran out the door to meet the new Santa. Looking at the boots she left behind, she's not even wearing a matching pair."

New Santa? One elf short? I'd think one of the twins' books had come to life if Cole's wife, Blaire, wasn't in charge of planning the Holly Ridge–Winterberry Glen Holiday Festival. I stare longingly for a second at the couch and fuzzy blanket I intended to burrito myself in this afternoon. But Netflix and the indent from my ass in the couch cushion I planned to deepen will be here when I get back. No further explanation needed, I grab my coat and the keys to my Bronco.

A wail sounds closer to the microphone on his side of the call. "Melody's weighing in. She really wants Uncle Austin to help out her mommy."

"Well, if Melody wants me to, how can I say no?" The front door to my apartment shuts firmly behind me, and I jog down the stairs to head to the street.

"You're already on your way, aren't you? And here I am breaking out the twin guilt."

"Well, you know me. I'll do anything for my godchildren." My voice holds a sarcastic tone, but I mean it to my core. I still expect Blaire and Cole to tell me, "Just kidding, we found a better role model," even though it has been six months since they asked me to fill the role of godfather to their kids.

"Uncle Austin's the best." Cole's voice holds a singsong tone that never fails to put a smile on my face and an ache in my gut. He's a great dad.

"Blaire will meet you at the high school so you can change into the costume and head over to the town square. Her assistant is doing crowd control with Santa until you get there."

My SUV roars to life, and I climb back out, tucking the phone between my shoulder and ear, letting the inside heat up while I scrape the windshield.

"There's never a dull moment with this holiday festival, is there?" I ask, reflecting on the fact that five years ago, my best friend was a certified Grinch. Now? He's married to the biggest Christmas lover who heads up the planning for the holiday festival our towns put on every year. A feat in its own right, this year is complicated even further by Blaire returning from maternity leave only two weeks before Thanksgiving and therefore two weeks before the festival started. Cole's mostly a stay-at-home parent right now and adjusting to life as a family of four has added its own brand of chaos to the mix, on top of everything the festival brings on its own.

"Maybe once the twins can take on volunteer roles, we'll be able to sleep again between Halloween and New Year's," he says, the fondness of his new life outweighing the exhaustion in his voice.

I snort, sliding into the front seat and clipping the phone onto the mount attached to the dashboard. "Keep telling yourself that, Dad. Let Blaire know I'll be there in fifteen minutes. Ten if I don't come across any lords-a-leaping on my way there."

"You're the best," Cole says.

"I know." I turn onto the Main Street of Winterberry Glen, heading to the bridge that takes me over to Holly Ridge. "Give the girls a kiss for me."

We hang up, and I turn the seat warmer down and the radio up, grateful it's early enough in the day traffic isn't crawling through this part of town. Eleven minutes later, I pull into the Holly Ridge High School parking lot and head into the gymnasium serving as festival headquarters.

A scene of organized chaos unfolds in front of me. People I recognize from both Holly Ridge and Winterberry Glen move around each other. Cindy from Winterberry Glen's grocery store carries a four-foot candy cane in each hand, a garland crown resting on top of her long, dark braids. Harold from the Holly Ridge Gazette pushes a cart of boxes marked "fragile" at a frightening speed, narrowly avoiding a crash with the woman I'm here to see. Blaire's buried in her phone, a clipboard tucked under her arm and what I'm certain is a Jitter's Peppermint Mocha in her hand. Her gait is slightly uneven from her mismatched boots, but she walks quickly across the floor to stop in front of me.

"Austin!" She wraps her arm around me, her cell phone tapping me on the back. I lean down to press a kiss to the top of her head before pulling back. "Did Cole tell you you're the best and a lifesaver? He was supposed to make that very clear."

"He definitely got the general sentiment across. What happened with the elf? And there's a new Santa?"

Blaire rolls her eyes and lets out a snort of frustrated breath. "The elf sprained their ankle in the Ice Town obstacle course last night. And what's worse, they took our Santa down with them and broke his collarbone in the process. They'll both be fine, but you can't very well tell a five-year-old Santa can't lift them onto his lap because his arm's in a sling, can you?"

I cover my mouth until I get my facial expression under control, picturing an elf and Santa dogpiled on the obstacle course. "Well, at least no one suffered any long-term injuries. And you should update the contract next year to say they can't partici-pate in any risky festival activities until after their duties are fulfilled."

Blaire snaps her fingers and points at me, her eyes shining. "Great idea, A. Thanks for that. Fits in an elf costume *and* comes with contract update ideas. Is there anything you can't do?"

My mouth opens, and even I'm not sure what self-deprecating thing will come out. A crash from the far corner draws our attention. Blaire's eyes shut tight. "I'm not going to look at what made that noise until I've got you settled. C'mon."

She weaves back through the crowds to the wall closest to us. The area outside the locker rooms is set up like a cross between a fitting room and a clothing store, with more empty hangers than full ones hanging on the coat rack at this point in the day.

Blaire flicks through the few elf costumes remaining, muttering to herself. "No, no. Damn it, I swore . . . ah ha!" She pulls down a green tunic with red accents and a pair of red and white striped bottoms. "Five-eleven to six-two. Perfect." She holds it out to me, proud of herself for finding one that will fit. Only a lifetime of love for Cole and an appreciation for how happy he and Blaire make each other stops me from grimacing as I take it from her.

"That'll work," I say, my eyes straying to the woman at the costume repair station behind Blaire, who hasn't stopped checking me out since we walked over. "But I'm at the top of that range. These bottoms might need to be let out in the crotch if this is going to be a long-term thing." I wink, and the woman's eyes stray to the area in question appreciatively.

"Stop it," Blaire says, whacking me in the arm with her clipboard.

I waggle my eyebrows at her. "What? An elf's not allowed to mingle and have a little fun?"

"Not while you're holding or wearing an elf costume, you're not. You're portraying the picture of wholesomeness for the kids, please. Now, go change." She plops a set of long johns in my hands and shoves me gently toward the locker room. "Put these on too. Santa's Workshop is heated, but with the door opening and closing you'll benefit from an extra layer."

I salute and make my way into the locker room, depositing my jacket into one of the lockers. I change quickly, not wanting to keep Blaire waiting longer than I have to. On my way out the door, I catch sight of myself in the mirror. "Not half bad, Owens," I mutter, fixing the messy locks of my dark brown hair into some sort of order. The green makes my blue-grey eyes pop, and my broad shoulders and muscular legs fill out every inch of stretch this costume has. While I was being a smartass flirting with the woman out there, the compression of the long johns under these leggings *does* help with Blaire's goal of presenting a wholesome elven image.

The door pops open a crack, and Blaire's voice sounds from outside the door. "I love you, but can you stop worrying about your hair and get out here? You're going to have to put on a hat anyway."

I laugh to myself and, taking one last look, make my way back out into the gymnasium. Blaire's waiting on the other side of the door with a hat and shoes that curl up at the toes, outfitted with a bell at each point.

"Hope the jingling shoes don't mess up your game." Blaire smirks as she hands them to me and starts leading me across the gym to a different door than the one I came in. "They'll slip on over your shoes, so you can put them on outside Santa's Workshop and not get them soaked."

"Blaire, please. I've been upping my squat game the past few months, practicing so I can hold both twins at once as they grow. These leggings on this ass can outweigh anything you throw at me, even elf hats or shoes with bells. My game is fine."

"That's the spirit," Blaire says. We reach the back of Santa's Workshop and she unlocks a door hidden behind a huge stack of presents and a Christmas tree. "Now, hat on, shoes jingling. Let's go make some kids' days."

We walk into the small hut, and my senses are inundated all at once. There's the smell of gingerbread and peppermint in the air, the warmth from the heating system, the potentially hazardous amount of twinkle lights strung around the room. And then, over the Christmas music playing at a low volume, I hear it. The booming laugh that feels like it's just ended when I wake up alone in the middle of the night, even after all this time. It can't be.

"Austin?" Blaire's voice is concerned, but fades into the background as I walk around the false wall separating Santa's chair from the back door.

One look confirms it. It is him. There, in a red suit and close-cropped beard he didn't have the last time I saw him, with rosy cheeks and twinkling eyes, is the owner of that laugh. The ghost of would-be Christmases past and broken futures—Brody Walker.

Chapter 2

Brody

The boy on my lap is listing the fifth video game he wants for the new gaming console he's asked for when a chill enters the room. The door at the front of the workshop hasn't opened. It must be the back entrance and the elf they're bringing to replace the reluctant stand-in who's been here since we opened an hour ago. She's "only temporary" and "has to get back to the gym"—she only mentioned it about five times before we let the families start filing in.

"Ahem." The noise comes from my knee, and I turn my full attention back on Carson Rose, age six.

"Sorry, Carson. I got a late start to Holly Ridge from the North Pole last night. Once you're done telling me the rest of what you want for Christmas, I hope you can help me."

Carson's eyes go wide. "I'm done. How can I help?"

"Well, I could sure use a big hug and a promise you'll be extra good for the rest of the year. It'll give me a big boost of energy."

"Sure!" Carson wraps his arms around me, and I sense rather than see his mom snapping a picture of the moment. "Thanks for listening, Santa. My mom told me Santa's budget is smaller than the new Switch, but I thought it doesn't hurt to ask." I make eye contact with his mom and notice the dark circles under her eyes and the slightly worn nature of her coat. A top rule of being a professional Santa? Never promise any major gifts.

"I think you're going to have a great Christmas, Carson. Be sure to tell your mom to stop by the Snowflake stand on the way out and grab yourselves some cookies, okay? Make sure your mom asks for one with sprinkles on it." I make eye contact with his mom and see her nod, confusion clear on her face.

Part of what my Santa company brings to anywhere we do visits for the public are special "sprinkle" cookies for adults. Those bags have a QR code inside they can scan and sign up to get some help during the holiday season. Assistance can come in the form of a gift card for groceries, winter clothes, or a present under the tree. It's one of the things I'm most proud of about my business.

Carson runs off back to his mother. I take a sip of water before greeting the next child, my mind wandering to how I ended up here. When the emergency Santa call came out for the Holly Ridge–Winterberry Glen Holiday Festival, I made sure the organizer, Blaire, didn't have time to consider anyone else. This means I've been awake for going on thirty hours, making arrangements to fill in the other bookings I had for the next several weeks. I'm pretty sure my assistant Monica aged about five years with all the last-minute changes. And then I had to get myself up here from New York City.

A small girl with brown skin and round brown eyes approaches me next. I snap back into Santa mode and push aside thoughts of whether I'll be able to make it over to Winterberry Glen tonight. Farah is telling me about the kitten she'd like for Christmas when I feel it. The weight of the gaze I'm not sure I deserve to feel again. I look to my right, and there he is. He's bulkier, and his brown hair is longer, curling over his forehead and above his ears from under his elf hat. He's pale, like he's seen a ghost.

Seeing him freezes me in place. I've imagined this moment so many times and in so many ways. But I never picture me wearing this suit and him wearing bells on his shoes and striped leggings. Blaire walks up to him and tugs on his arm, her face full of concern. He lets her pull him behind the fake wall at my back.

Farah tugs on my beard, and I thank the Santa gods I perfected the art of whitening my real facial hair years ago. I turn my attention back to her, cursing the terrible Santa I'm being today. "Yes, Farah, I'm sorry. You were telling me about the kitten you want." I glance up at her mom, who nods her head and smiles, letting me know they're all in on this particular wish. "What do you think you'll name her?"

This sets off a list of name options, dependent on fur and eye color combos. I smile, nod, and do my Santa laugh at appropriate intervals. Farah gives me a hug and we pose for a photo before she runs off, regaling her parents with every reaction and smile I gave her.

Blaire walks up and addresses the crowd. "Santa needs a milk and cookie break, everyone. He'll be back in five!" She gestures for me to follow her, and the temporary elf comes along too.

As soon as we're hidden from view, Blaire turns to the other woman with us. "Lexie, I'm really sorry, but you're going to need to stay here for the rest of the day."

My heart sinks to my feet as I look around and realize Austin's nowhere to be seen. He took one look at me and ran out on the elf gig? Why is he an elf anyway?

Lexie sputters, but the back door opening again interrupts her. Austin walks back into the workshop, his coloring returned to normal, and his expression schooled and neutral.

"Oh, Austin. I'm just telling Lexie she'll need to—"

He cuts her off. "It's okay, B. I told you, I only needed a minute. I'm good."

My eyes bounce between the two, trying to figure out what Blaire knows about me. I've never allowed myself to search for Austin online in all the years we've been apart until he popped up in a video on the festival's social media account last year—as a professional Santa, my algorithm is very predictable. From there,

I've tried to limit the time I spend on his accounts, but there isn't a lot for us Santas to do over the summer, leaving a lot of time to scroll. Blaire started popping up on his accounts around five years ago, with and without his best friend, Cole. And Cole—he knows exactly who I am.

"Well, okay," she says, her tone sounding unsure. "I meant to call a short break to introduce you two, but it seems you already know each other."

Austin's speaking before I've come close to imagining what to say. "Well, I wouldn't say *know* each other, but yes, Brody and I have met."

My eyes close briefly, flashes from ten years ago I'd locked away breaking free. Austin and I laughing together, eating together, being together. The welcome to Winterberry Glen sign in my rearview mirror as I drove away. A deep inhale in, and my eyes open to find Austin watching me, his look of concern quickly morphing back into one of disinterest as soon as our gazes meet.

"Yes. We've met," I say in return, not willing to look away first. The Christmas music and sounds of eager small voices filter in from the other side of the wall. Austin's blue-grey eyes see deep inside me and look through me all at once, before they blink and look back at Blaire. I follow suit and see her looking between us, wringing her hands.

"I'm too sleep-deprived for this, so if you all are good for today, we'll go with it. Brody, why don't you get back out there? Lexie, you can give Austin a rundown of what he needs to know, and then I'll meet you back in the gym."

We all nod in agreement. I take a second to be sure my suit is straight and hat is appropriately jaunty before taking a deep breath and heading back to my chair and the waiting children.

I sit down, and a young Vietnamese boy steps up, next in line. Hands tucked behind his back, he keeps shooting furtive looks at me and then looking back down.

"Hi there. What's your name?" My smile breaks wide across my face, doing my best to be approachable. I lean on my leg to get close to his level, careful not to extend too much into his space. The number of kids who start out excited about meeting Santa and then freeze up when it's their turn has taught me a lot of tricks over the years.

"Quang," he mumbles, his gaze meeting mine for longer this time before his cheeks redden and he looks back down.

"Hi, Quang. You can call me Nick, if you'd like." He looks up in surprise, and I shoot him a wink. His face lights up with the special joy only experienced by children at Christmastime, and he steps closer to me, keeping eye contact as he stands next to my knee.

"Would you like to come up and sit on my knee to tell me what you'd like for Christmas? Or do you want to stay there?"

He nods and breaks into an elaborate description of the art set he'd like. My gaze never strays from him, but I sense rather than see Austin come to stand next to me. I find so much joy in playing Santa for all these kids who still believe in the magic of Christmas, and that's enough to keep me engaged on a regular day. But knowing Austin's here now, and will see me in my element? My energy levels rise, and I vow to be the best damn Santa he's ever seen.

After we pose for photos, I turn back to the young boy clinging onto my red velvet pants. "Thanks for visiting me today, Quang. I hope you have a great Christmas. My friend Austin here will help you get back to your mom."

Quang sticks his hand out for Austin to take, a different child than the shy one who approached me. Austin reaches toward him, and a whiff of his spicy cologne follows as he crosses into my space for the first time today. I watch for a moment, heart in my eyes and lead in my stomach as Quang regales Austin with the details of his art set too while they walk back to his mom.

A blond girl with long braids steps up onto the stool placed next to my chair to help them settle on my knee, and my attention returns to the task at hand—listening to these kids and giving them their special moment with Santa. I even I direct Austin to help some of the older ones who could walk back to their parents on their own. He never meets my eye, but the whiff of spices I get each time he comes close is too addicting to give up. I catch him smiling and even hear him bark out a laugh before swallowing it when one little boy asks for an underwater trampoline. We fall into a rhythm. Between visitors, a fleeting thought crosses my mind. In all the dreams I had about Austin and me reuniting, I never considered a scenario of him being a part of this with me. Even if I had, and even though he won't look at me, I don't know I could have come close to getting it right. Austin Owens is the type of man to burrow deep inside you and, no matter how hard you try to dig him out, will always leave traces of himself behind.

Chapter 3

Austin

If I'm being honest, I expected my time as an elf to crawl by. When I found out the festival's new Santa was none other than Brody—crusher of hearts and dreams—those four hours should have moved like molasses.

But instead, the time flies by. I'm careful to avoid Brody's eyes, not wanting him to catch any of my tangled emotions at his being the new Santa, being *here*. I have to admit it, he's a fucking fantastic Santa Claus. How the hell he went from his dreams of being a high-powered litigator to this, I have no idea. It's killing me not knowing this about him, but I won't allow myself to ask. It's a lot safer if I don't allow myself to know anything about who he is now.

One of the other elves in the workshop shuts the door behind the last family, sliding the deadbolt firmly in place. Suddenly, the space that's been full of dozens of people all day feels too small for the two of us to share. I look around, not sure what my role is in cleaning anything up. No one's paying me any attention, not even Brody, who's speaking with the elf behind the cookie and photo counter. I take it as my opportunity to slip out undetected, removing my jingle shoes as quietly as possible and sneaking out the back door. It's dark outside. The lights decorating the festival market stalls twinkle in the cold air with scents of mulled wine and roasted nuts drifting over from across the way. But there's no time to be distracted by Christmas goodness. I speed walk the distance across the town square to the gym, throwing up a prayer to whoever might be listening I can get changed and out of here before Brody makes his way to the locker room.

No such luck. I have my flannel shirt back on, but I pull down the leggings and long johns right as the door to the locker room opens and Brody makes his way inside, all five feet, eleven inches of him, encased in red velvet.

His eyes dart immediately to the part of my body now only covered by my candy-cane-striped boxer briefs. I fight the urge to cover myself, cursing I didn't get my pants on faster. He looks away, his cheeks growing a darker pink under the edges of his beard. My own face heats, and I roll my eyes at myself internally. It's a locker room, and while it's been a decade, the man who just walked in has seen all of me in much less than what I'm wearing now. I turn my back on Brody, thanking my trainer and his relentless focus on squats. I know that has my ass looking plump. I manage to take my leggings the rest of the way off and step into my jeans.

"Ahem." Brody clears his throat once I have pants back in place. It seems I'm not getting out of here without some sort of interaction, so it's time to face the music.

After I grab my coat and jam my feet back into my shoes, I can't delay any longer. I gather up my costume and face his direction. It's my turn to take in the parts of Brody's body he's uncovered as he de-Santifies himself. He's removed the coat and pillow popping out of his bowl-full-of-jelly belly, resting them both on the bench next to him. But my eyes trace a rounder stomach than he had the last time I saw him, reminiscent of the photos he showed me of an adolescent Brody. By the time I met him, he had his eyes set on corporate law and held tightly to the notion that a certain type of physique would best serve him to get there. Even now, when my gym time is at an all-time high to fill the empty holes in my schedule, it doesn't match what Brody would wake up at 4:30 a.m. to do most days.

My hand twitches, longing to stroke the soft curve of his stomach, the magnetic draw between us still as strong now as ten years ago. I give myself an internal shake. The times when I got to touch Brody however I wanted are long gone.

He clears his throat again, and I wonder how long I've been standing here silent, taking him in. Whatever he intended to say after his initial attention-getting seems long gone.

"So, hi," he says. My eyes *do* roll now. Ten years and "So, hi," is what he goes with? I walk toward him, the bells on the shoes stuffed under my arm jingling with each step I take.

"What are you doing here, Brody?" The elf hat I only now realized I'm still wearing, along with the jingling bells probably undercut the impassive expression I'm trying to keep on my face, like the sight of him after all this time doesn't gut me.

"I'm . . . I'm here to fill-in for the festival's Santa." For someone who argues for a living, Brody looks off-balance at the venom in my voice. Or is it argued? He can't still be at a firm if he's here to be Santa for the rest of the festival.

"There have to be a million Santa openings across the Northeast this time of year. Pick one, and leave without looking back. You're good at that," I say.

Brody's shoulders roll back. Even through my anger and hurt at seeing him, I have to admit the determined look works on Santa's— well at least on Santa Brody's—face.

"But no other Santa job brings me back to you."

The force of his words collides with me like a physical thing, and I take a step backward. I open my mouth searching for something to say. Coming up empty, I do what I should have done as soon as I changed. I head for the door.

"Austin, wai—"

The door swinging shut behind me cuts off his words. I take a few deep breaths, counting on the fact he won't follow until he's out of his suit. By then, I plan to be long gone.

I spot Blaire across the gym. Dropping my costume in the laundry cart, I make my way to her.

"Austin, I'm so sorry. I had no idea Brody was *the guy.*"

I wince. "Talked to Cole, have you?"

She nods, not even bothering to look ashamed. And it's fine, really, I would have told her if Cole didn't. She deserves to know why I almost bailed on her this afternoon.

"Why don't you head over to the house for dinner and twin snuggles?"

I start to protest. The last thing they need to do is pick up my pieces when they're still figuring out how they all fit together as a family of four.

She holds up her hand to interrupt me. "Cole insists, and so do I. Plus, it's been what, a week since you've seen the girls? They've grown inches and inches, I swear." Her eyes flick behind me, and whatever she sees inspires her "no arguments" face. "I have to walk Brody over to the apartment above Jitters, and he's about to head this way. So you can either stand here and argue with me, or you can get your ass moving, Owens."

I nod, knowing a lost cause when I see one. "Okay, I'll see you at your place in a little bit."

She squeezes my arm, and I walk out of the gym, fighting myself all the way not to look back.

I let myself into Cole and Blaire's house only a few blocks away from Holly Ridge. I learned the hard way not to let myself in unannounced after they bought this place and moved in, but also learned the *harder* way that ringing the doorbell and announcing myself when it's possible one or both babies is sleeping risks banishment.

"Honey, I'm home," I whisper, walking carefully into the

living room. Cole is dozing in the armchair, and I tiptoe toward the double bassinet next to him. Cassidy and Melody are both miraculously asleep at the same time. I leave them all to their snoozing and head to the kitchen. After grabbing a beer from the fridge and taking a long drag from the glass bottle, I roll up my sleeves and get started on the world's quietest dishwasher emptying.

"You don't have to do that," Cole says, and I jump, nearly dropping the plate in my hand. The relieved look on his face tells me everything I need to know about how the day went.

"I'm not sure when three people last slept at the same time in this house, so I didn't want to disturb you. Plus, apparently, you're feeding me tonight. Figure I can earn my keep."

Cole doesn't argue, and I put the last of the silverware away while he grabs a beer of his own from the fridge. He jerks his head for me to follow him through the dining room and into his office. I smirk when I spot a small Christmas tree has been put up since I last came in here. Cole plops into one of the armchairs next to the fireplace and puts his beer and the baby monitor on the table between us.

"So, how are you?"

"I'm jingle-riffic. Why would you ask?" My own flop into the chair is too heavy to hide my lie, not that Cole would believe me anyway. He levels me with a look, and I take another sip for bravery.

"Of all the things on my list of possibilities to happen today, Brody Walker being here wasn't one of them," I say, reclining my head so I'm staring at the orbs cast on the ceiling by the tree lights.

"I mean, you haven't heard from him in what, ten years?"

"Nine years, five months, and twenty-four days." I roll my neck so I'm looking at Cole again, his expression exactly what I expected. A mix of pity and reproach. "What? He left on the first of the month. It's not *that* hard to keep count."

"We'll blow right past that for now," he continues. "Why did you stick around? Blaire said she thought you bailed for a minute —she wouldn't have blamed you if you had."

I shrug. "I knew if you called to recruit me to help, Blaire was in a real bind. Plus, I didn't want to give him the satisfaction of knowing he got to me. I mean, he probably still knows, but this way he doesn't have me running away as proof. Besides, he's the runner, not me."

We sit in the quiet for a moment, a coo from one of the girls lighting up the monitor the only thing breaking the silence.

"So, he's here for the rest of the—"

"Yep," I say, draining the rest of the bottle. "I'm going to need another one of these. Can I get you one?"

Cole shakes his head. "I'm not even sure I'll finish this one, but I didn't want you to drink alone. Help yourself. You can always sleep on the couch if you need to."

The reality that I have no reason to wake up early requiring me to be home and in bed at a reasonable time hits me. I grab another local Christmas ale from the fridge to push the thought away. Fuck, there's a dark road if I let myself go down it.

"Can you grab me a Diet Coke?" Blaire whispers from behind me, and I almost shatter something breakable in this kitchen for the second time tonight.

"Jesus, you guys are quiet," I say, opening the fridge again and grabbing a can from the door.

"I think the ability to tiptoe unlocks somewhere around the fifth night in a row you see three a.m." She cracks the can and winces at the loud noise it makes. After a beat of silence, she lets out a breath. "I ordered from Joe's, food should be here in a—"

The sound of the doorbell interrupts her sentence, and we swear in unison. She heads for the living room, but I redirect her to the front door. "We've got them."

Right on cue, Cole is in the kitchen, dropping a quick peck on his wife's mouth before following me into the living room.

"Hi, Melody." I pick her up and she stops crying, her eyes wide as she stares at my face. "That's right, Uncle Austin's got the magic touch." I bounce her lightly as I walk to the kitchen. Blaire drops the bags on the table.

"I don't know how many more delivery drivers this town has we haven't yelled at in the last four months, but there's one less now," she says, grabbing two pre-measured bottles off the counter and mixing them, one in each hand.

"If I didn't know how biology worked, I might think that's how you got into this situation in the first place," I say, looking at her double jack-off motions meaningfully.

She rolls her eyes and doesn't bother responding, reaching for Melody.

"That's fair. Not my best work. I can feed her if you'd rather have a hot meal for once. But I know you've been gone all day."

Blaire smiles, her arms still out, so I hand over her daughter. "I've gotten pretty good at eating one-handed once they burp. If you want to grab stuff to serve, that would be great."

I nod, giving Melody's head one last brush before heading to the cupboards to grab what we need.

"I sent an email to all the festival volunteers and employees before I left the gym asking if anyone could pick up the extra elf shifts," Blaire says over the sounds of two girls enthusiastically enjoying their dinner. "I'm worried it still won't be enough. Word's already spreading about how great our new Santa is— we're booked for the next week solid and there are already emails asking if we'll open up more spots."

I'm glad I'm facing away from them, so they can't see the mixture of emotions I know dash across my face. Happiness that Brody will bring so much to the festival, pain at hearing how good he is, and worry I'm about to do something stupid.

It's been silent for a long while, and I turn around to find Blaire and Cole engaged in some sort of silent conversation. Guess there's no getting out of talking about this.

"Guys, it's fine. You're my best friends. My ex is playing an integral role in the festival, and it sounds like he's going to be a huge draw. He's going to come up. I'm fine."

"Can you say it without a wounded, sad Austin look in your eyes?" Blaire asks, concern clear in hers. I sigh, but can't fight the smile at how fiercely my best friend's wife cares about the people she loves.

"I'll work on it." I pull the containers out of the paper bag and start scooping pasta and salad onto our plates. The girls are blissed out, milk drunk. I get back up to grab burp cloths for each of them, grabbing my beer from where I left it on the counter.

"Well, luckily you're booked up at Sullivan's for the rest of the season," Blaire says, scooping a bite of pasta into her mouth before adjusting the baby upright and patting her back gently. "That gives you an ironclad out, if even a fraction of you feels like avoiding your ex isn't reason enough."

My eyes stay trained on my plate. Getting the perfect dressing to salad ratio suddenly needs all my attention.

"Austin," she says, forcing me to look at her. "You still have Sullivan's, right?"

I lean back in my chair, running my hand through my hair. "They always do staffing cuts after the fall festival ends at Halloween, before they transition to the tree farm. The oldest O'Neil kid was on the list to lose his job, and apparently his dad's on the road until the New Year, and the baby had to go to the emergency room . . ." I trail off, my eyes bouncing between my best friends' eyes, finding a mixture of pity and fondness.

"What? He doesn't have his license, and he can walk to the farm. I have a license and a reliable vehicle, so I rideshare and do food delivery. It'll be fine. You know there's always someone willing to hire me over in the Glen. I need to figure out what I want to do next." I've worked at most of the businesses around Winterberry Glen in one capacity or another, whether directly or providing a service there from somewhere else. It works well for how quickly I get restless.

Cole clears his throat. "You'll definitely find something else soon. And I'm sure with everyone visiting both towns for the festival, there's a lot of rides and orders to pick up. But since Halloween, Austin? It's been three weeks."

"Okay, Dad. You have enough going on with your actual kids. You didn't need to worry about your grown-up-best-friend kid."

"I mean, yeah, I'm worried, but it's not—" Blaire lays her hand on his arm, and he takes a deep breath. "Just because the girls are here doesn't mean I don't want to know about your life, have you over for a beer, and watch twenty minutes of TV at a time."

"I know, man." And I do know he means it, to his core. But I also know a person only has so much emotional capacity, and I can take care of myself.

We sit in silence for a few moments, eating dinner and looking at our phones. Fuck, I made it awkward when they didn't even need to have me over in the first place.

"Fuck," Blaire mutters, startling the rest of us, but luckily, no one starts crying and the adults laugh instead. "No one can take on extra shifts."

Cole's eyes meet mine, and he shakes his head ever so slightly. I shrug and he smiles, his head shaking fondly this time.

"What? I'm too tired to interpret whatever's happening here," Blaire says, no longer fazed that Cole and I can do the silent talking thing, too.

"I'll take the elf job," I say, picking up everyone's plates and heading to the sink.

"Austin, no, I can't let you." She gets up and comes to stand next to me. I turn around, my back to the counter so I can see them both.

"You need someone to cover, I need steady income, and some closure might be nice. So I have to be around my ex six or so days a week for the next month. It won't kill me."

Blaire silently hands me Melody. She pats me on the shoulder, the way one might an animal who just ungracefully fell off a piece of furniture, before hip checking me out of the way so she can do the dishes, telling me she thinks it just might.

$$Chapter\ 4$$

Brody

Santa's Workshop doesn't open until noon on weekdays. That doesn't mean I plan on sleeping in though. I often find it difficult to sleep my first night in a new place, so I expect to be up before the sun—a habit I've struggled to break even since I stopped practicing law. When my eyes crack open, the time on the microwave clock says it's just after 8:00 a.m. Though, I suppose I shouldn't be surprised. 2:00 a.m. came and went with me still awake because I couldn't stop thinking of the way Austin's ass looked in those leggings. And, in a more depressing reality, the way his face hardened when he reminded me I walked away from him without looking back.

I stretch, and roll out of bed, wincing as my feet hit the cold floor. I add slippers to the mental list of things I'll need to grab at some store, sometime. Middle of the night last-minute packing means some things are going to end up left behind. Unintentionally left behind and forgotten. The exact opposite of what I've done with Austin, despite my best intentions.

After taking a piss, swallowing my morning meds, and adding slippers to the actual list on my phone, I unroll my yoga mat. I logged into YouTube on the SmartTV last night and now see my favorite YouTube instructor uploaded a new Christmas-themed flow. The next thirty minutes pass in the blink of an eye as I center myself and get ready for the day ahead.

After the video wraps with one of the most peaceful versions of *O Christmas Tree* I've ever heard, I roll up the mat and get ready to shower for the day. I started doing yoga in the months after I left the firm. Giving up my old gym routine was easy enough, but I like the way yoga keeps me moving my body in a more forgiving way and helps to quiet my thoughts. During the other ten months of the year, I alternate between the studio down the block from my house and more traditional videos. But during Santa season? Something about starting the day with a Christmas-themed routine really gets my jolly jumping.

Post-shower, I stand at the mirror wrapped in a towel. The hair coloring powder I use to turn my beard and hair an acceptable more salt-than-pepper combo sits on the sink. As I comb it through and let it set, I stare at the reflection looking back at me. Blue eyes, ready to twinkle. Relatively neat, trimmed beard being a Santa under forty lets me get away with. Round cheeks with a tendency to turn pink much easier than I would like.

My eyes trail downward, eyeing the dark chest hair I've stopped shaving. The darkening trail disappears under my towel, which no longer falls flat like it used to, but curves out with the flesh of my stomach. Acceptance of my body's natural burly and stocky form came hand in hand with the work my therapist and I did to unwrap my guilt at leaving the career I worked so hard for, but found such little fulfillment in.

If Austin had been surprised when he saw me without my full suit on, he hid it well. My towel starts to rise a little more as I remember the heat in his eyes as he took me in, his gaze like a ghost of all the touches we shared before.

Shaking myself, I test the powder on my beard, which should be fully set by now. My hand comes back free of residue, which means I'm free to get dressed and get on with my day. Pulling on my clothes, I wonder how I'll see Austin again. From my internet stalking, it looks like the place he's been working at during the fall holds a bustling Christmas tree farm in the same location. Yesterday's favor must have been on one of his days off.

Suit garment bag slung over my arm, I make my way carefully down the outside stairs leading from the studio apartment Blaire arranged for me to stay in. Apparently, one of the perks of staying in this particular location includes a daily allotment of coffee and pastries. Trying to get Austin off my mind last night led to a deep dive into their holiday festival-themed menu. I can't wait to try most of the drinks on offer, so I can pick a favorite.

"Welcome to Jitters!" someone calls as I walk through the door, hit with a wall of warmth and the smells of fresh ground coffee and baked goods. This may ruin me for other Santa jobs.

"Brody!" Susie smiles at me from behind the counter. She met Blaire and me last night at the apartment and gave me the lay of the land while Blaire ran off to get home to something.

"Hi there, Susie. Tell me, which do you like better? The Eggnog Latte or the Gingerbread Macchiato?" Considering the products she stocks the bathroom with upstairs, I have a pretty good guess.

Susie doesn't disappoint. "The Gingerbread Macchiato. Sometimes I make it for myself in July as a little pick-me-up."

I smile, feeling a kindred spirit with a fellow Christmas lover. "I'll take one of those, please, and a bacon and egg croissant."

She gives my order to one of the runners and looks at me appraisingly.

"I feel like I've seen you around before." My face must look as confused as I think it does, because she laughs. "Before last night, I mean."

"Oh. I lived in Winterberry Glen for about eighteen months a decade ago."

"Oh, and here I thought you only swung by every December twenty-fourth." She winks at someone to my right, and I look down to see a young girl around seven studying me carefully. I give her a wink too, and put my finger to my mouth, indicating she should keep me being here a secret. My gaze returns to Susie to find her looking like she just ate a canary. "But thanks for confirming the rumors."

These blasted cheeks of mine heat right on cue, and her smile softens. "It would have passed by unnoticed five years ago. But since *he's* best friends with the husband of one of Holly Ridge's shining gems, he filters through the gossip mill more and more. Plus, the feud between the towns is mostly old news now. A wider whisper network."

My cheeks burn even warmer. There's no pretending I don't know which "he" Susie's referring to. My heart warms right along with them though, hearing how Holly Ridge regards Austin as such a staple around town, like Winterberry Glen does.

She hands me a paper cup of coffee and a white bag holding my sandwich. I know I need to let her get back to work, but find myself saying, "I wondered what changed. I remember the Christmas festival, but when I saw it rebranded as the Holly Ridge–Winterberry Glen Holiday Festival, I almost thought somewhere else had stolen your names."

"You should ask him about it. He was there, he knows all the insider details."

All the warmth at the mention of Austin goes out at the reminder of my current situation. "Oh, I don't know about that. I'm not even sure when I'll see him again."

Susie gestures out the window with her chin. I follow the path of her gaze in time to see Austin walk past the café. He's headed toward the gym. "You never know what those Christmas elves will rustle up for the right person."

Her cheer and optimism are infectious and the locked-up organ in my chest starts to hope. Maybe this isn't a foolhardy, overly-impulsive plan after all. I lift my cup in thanks. "Well, I better get this breakfast eaten and get myself ready for another day of spreading cheer."

"I'll be sure we have an Eggnog Latte and egg sandwich ready for you at eleven tomorrow."

I thank Susie again and head back out into the cold, annoyed that carrying my suit means I can't dig into this sandwich emitting smells from heaven. After pushing my way into the locker room, I peek down a couple of the rows of lockers, not seeing Austin anywhere. I guess he had another destination after all.

With my suit safely hung in one of the lockers, I sit myself down to enjoy my breakfast. A moan even I have to admit sounds a bit orgasmic leaves my lips after the first bite. It's going to be hard to try any other sandwiches on the menu when the croissants are this good.

"Susie's are good, but the ones from Buzzed over in the Glen are better." Austin's voice startles me so much the sandwich falls out of my hand and lands at my feet. I stare at it, telling myself repeatedly I can't pick it up off a high school locker room floor and eat it.

"Fuck," I say, taking my drink and holding it with both hands. I can't lose two things so closely together.

"Now, would Santa really have that kind of a mouth on him?" Austin says, walking over to stand in front of me. He holds out a white bag, a familiar scent wafting out of it.

"Oh no, I can't take your breakfast," I say. "I have some protein bars in the pocket of my garment bag. I'll have—"

The bag shakes in my face, the smell increasing. "Blaire gave me this when I got here. I already had one from Buzzed on my way in. I don't need both, and Santa can't get hangry. Consider it a peace offering."

I look up at him, wary. "Just like that?"

He shrugs. "Once the shock wore off, I'm over it." He keeps his eyes steady on mine. The Austin I knew couldn't lie for shit and still held a grudge against his next-door neighbor for something from second grade. I take the bag from him.

"You're over it?" I feel like a parrot, repeating what he's saying. But yesterday, the looks he shot my way—when he bothered to acknowledge I existed—could freeze Winterberry Lake the whole way to the bottom.

"I'm over it." Austin's eyes dart once to his shoes, the same tell he's always had when he's lying. His eyes widen once he realizes I've caught it, and he whirls around, taking away my ability to read his expression.

"So, what are you doing here?" I ask his back.

"I've decided to lean into this new tights fetish I'm developing," he says, his tone dry. "I took the job. Blaire needs my help; I need the work. Shouldn't we get ready? Blaire said you wanted to be at the workshop at 11:30 to go over some reports? I'm your elf escort for today."

"Right," I catapult myself into action, finishing the last of the sandwich. I go to wash my hands, not wanting to touch my suit with greasy fingers. When I get back, Austin's leggings are on, and he's pulling the tunic top over a stomach with abs much more defined than the last time I saw him with his shirt off.

He clears his throat. We really need to stop getting caught staring at each other's stomachs. "So, uh, you take this Santa stuff really seriously, huh? Uh, what happened—"

His question is cut off by a few high school aged boys coming into the locker room. One whispers something to the other, which makes the second boy snicker. They move quickly to the stalls at the back of the space.

Austin and I finish getting ready in silence until the outer door shuts behind them again. By then, we're both ready to go and there's no sense in delaying any longer.

"After you, Santa," Austin says, holding the door and ushering me into the gym. I look around at the bustle of activity, something dawning on me.

"Wait, school's still in session, right? Massachusetts didn't change some law giving them off between Thanksgiving and New Year's? How can we be in their gym?"

He holds open the door to the outside, and we bundle our coats against the cold winter wind. "The students use their gym periods during the weeks between Thanksgiving and holiday break to help out with festival stuff—it gives them a community service unit on their transcripts. And besides, if there was a new law, wouldn't you know about it?" He waves at a few people as we make our way across the square, taking special care to greet the kids who point at us as we walk past.

"Not a lot of call for keeping up with K-12 Massachusetts educational laws in the corporate world," I say, my tone as bitter as the chill from the cold.

Austin shoots me a questioning look, but lets it go. "The community service thing was Blaire's idea. They used to coordinate out of a huge tent in the parking lot of the high school, which is not ideal for obvious weather reasons." He pulls his scarf up over his mouth, his words mumbled. "A lot of this is thanks to her."

I nod as we reach the back door to Santa's Workshop, and Austin pulls out a key, unlocking it and letting us inside. We both breathe a sigh of relief at the warmth. "She really seems like Superwoman. Cole's a lucky guy."

"Of course he is. An awesome wife and a great best friend. What more does he need? Well, I guess now—" The door opening cuts Austin off. A kid who barely looks eighteen walks in the door.

"Mr. Santa. Mr. Austin." He nods at both of us. "I'm Jimmy. Ms. Blaire sent me, said you were looking for someone to head up the cookie and picture station." My eyebrows rise. Jimmy rolls his eyes and keeps talking. "I know, I look fifteen, but I'm actually twenty-two. I'm finishing up my last semester at the community college, getting my non-profit management certificate. Ms. Blaire said you have a foundation that funds gifts for some of the kids who come through? She thought I'd be the perfect fit."

I stick out my hand to shake his. "It'll be great to have you, Jimmy. I prefer to have the same person running the stand when we can, to be sure the right information is being exchanged without the kids catching wind of anything. Come on over. I'll show you how it works."

Austin looks at me quizzically for a beat before shaking his head and heading off to check the bathroom is ready for the public. As Jimmy and I walk past the open bathroom door, I hear something that sounds a lot like a muttered, "I'm over it, goddamnit."

$$Chapter\ 5$$

Austin

I'm not over it.

Day three of playing elf to Brody's Santa dawns like most other days in New England this time of year: cold with low, grey clouds threatening snow. Yesterday's approach of pretending we have no history backfired on me. Brody's piercing blue eyes saw right through my bullshit. Fortunately, once we got into the workshop, the crowds Blaire predicted kept us too busy to have much interaction outside of the kids visiting the North Pole. Afterward, Brody and Jimmy posted up near the cookie station to talk more about his foundation's work. While they were distracted, I slipped out the back door and made it back to my car without encountering Brody again.

My shift is scheduled to start right before the workshop opens today. After I hang up my coat and make my way around the false wall, I'm struck still by the energy of my fellow North Pole-ers. The photographer is fluffing the snow around Brody's throne. Two of the elves on crowd control duty are hanging yet another strand of lights. And Brody and Jimmy are back at the stand again, hunched together looking at the screen.

A quick glance around tells me everything's under control. I find myself drifting toward the pair and their computer. The way Jimmy looks at Brody—that's hero worship, right? Brody has almost fifteen years on Jimmy, but who am I to judge? The last woman I picked up at Peppers outside of the Ridge was probably at least that much older than me, but I'd never ask a lady her age outright.

"But if you migrate everything into an Airtable here, you're able to join the records and filter for different views, which will make tracking a lot easier. Plus, automations will save time with follow-ups and communication." Jimmy is demonstrating some sort of database on the screen while Brody looks on.

"That's a really great idea, Jimmy. Would you have time to migrate us over in the next week or so? I can pay you outside of the festival's rate, too." Brody looks impressed.

"For sure. I can probably even get it done before we're back on Thursday with the day off tomorrow." Santa's Workshop closes every Wednesday to help ensure the staff actually get a day off. "Oh hey, Mr. Austin," Jimmy says, spotting me from where I lurk next to a lamppost wrapped in garland and surrounded by boxes of presents.

"Austin, hi," Brody says, turning to face me, his eyes lighting up as they land on me. It starts to warm my insides. I need to shut that shit down real fast.

"Hi," I say, trying to shove my hands in my pockets before I remember I'm wearing skin-tight leggings. I settle for crossing them instead. They both look at me, expecting me to continue, but I stay silent. The awkwardness grows.

"Well," Brody clears his throat and looks at his watch, "going to hit the head once more before we open. We'll talk more about your rate when we're done?" He looks at Jimmy, who nods, before walking past us, getting stopped by the photographer wanting his feedback on something.

I look back at Jimmy to find him watching me. "So, what's the deal there?"

"What? What deal? There's no deal." I sputter, making it so much worse.

Jimmy rolls his eyes at me. "Part of being good at fundraising is being able to read people and suss out connections and relationships. There's a deal there. Plus, you looked like you wanted to squeeze my head like a gumdrop when you walked over."

I gaze at him, assessing. The kid's young, but I see the truth in his eyes as he continues to stare at me.

"Well, if you're not going to tell me, I'll guess. You guys have a *history*, right?" He holds up his fingers to tick off his points. "Brody's in the third year of his Santa business, and he graduated *summa cum laude* from NYU four years before that, so it must have been a decade ago." My mouth drops open, and he shrugs. "What? I googled him. Needed to make sure all this do-goodedness is legit before I get too invested. I've been tricked before." His eyes stray to the screen as he switches back to grilling me about my relationship with Brody. "Must be pretty awkward, working this closely with an ex? Or did you guys part on good terms, you're just still horny for him?"

"Why did Brody start his Santa business?" I decide to answer his question with a question, not particularly interested in revealing any private parts of myself to this relative stranger.

Jimmy's eyes shoot up to mine. "So not good terms, then. But still horny for him. I don't know. Even if I did . . . I think that's something you should ask him yourself. But maybe not right now." He nods at something behind me, and I whirl around to find Brody walking back to us, coat fully buckled, black shoes shining, and hat jauntily sat on his head.

Brody's face is contemplative, like he wants to ask me something that might upset me. A quick glance at his watch seems to tell him we don't have time.

"Ready for another day?" he asks instead.

"I was born ready," I say, wincing at my weak response.

Brody smirks, his eyes gaining an extra sparkle, telling me he agrees it's not my best work. "Well then, Mr. Elf. Let's make some days."

I want to roll my eyes at his self-assuredness, but it's always been a big part of what attracted me to Brody. Never uncertain about his path or his future. Maybe the possibility of stability and steadiness is what really appealed to me. He knew what he wanted and wouldn't let anything get in the way of those goals. It turns out, not even someone he claimed to love.

The smile I flash at the first child off Brody's lap turns forced as my thoughts go to a dark place. The beginning of an eight-hour shift is not the time to think about how easily Brody cast me aside. I need to be projecting joy and Christmas cheer, not despair and loneliness.

I force myself to push away those thoughts, instead brainstorming what other presents I should get for the twins. But as time passes, I find myself needing less distraction and instead listening to the conversations Brody's having with the kids.

The festival attracts people from all over the tri-state area, but even locally, Holly Ridge and Winterberry Glen have diverse socioeconomic populations. This means the requests made to Santa vary just as widely. I know how hard my mom worked to hide any hardships from me. But when Santa brought some kids mp3 players and brought me a lot of socks and underwear, plus a toy or two, it wasn't hard to pick up on something being different.

The same is true of kids today, except some of these kids have a self-awareness and selflessness I didn't possess at their age. Alongside wishes for scooters and game systems are requests for new jobs for Mom or less time on the road for Dad. Brody's so good with them all, no difference in his reaction or expression if the kid's acting their age or displaying an emotional maturity far beyond their years. What is different is how he prompts those who ask for something outside of themselves to dig deep for a toy or game they want, too. And the way their eyes shine when Santa sees right to the heart of them is priceless.

Once again, I find myself reflecting on what a natural Brody is at this. He's patient and kind and gives his full attention to every child. This Brody is nothing like the paralegal destined for a prestigious law school and a long career in corporate law I knew. Or at least thought I did. I never thought the Brody I knew would abandon everything we planned together either. What else did I get wrong back then?

Finally, the door closes behind the last family arguing about whether it's too late to grab a cup of hot chocolate for the road.

Everyone starts to wrap things up for the night, moving with a speed indicating how much these folks need a day off. I, only on day three, instead wonder if I can force myself to wake up in time to do some food deliveries before Cole and I take the girls for a Christmas present related photo shoot. When I asked why he didn't bring the girls to the festival to see Santa, Cole let me know with a straight face Blaire would kill him if he took the girls to see Santa for the first time without her. A department store photo studio is a safe choice for the calendar gift he has in mind—twelve months of Christmas-themed photos.

Brody approaches me, the same pensive look on his face he had before we started, stopping all my schedule calculations. If the last eight hours of interacting with children didn't make him forget his question, it may be better to get it over with.

"I'm surprised you took the job."

Not a question after all. Whatever I expected him to say, it's not that.

"Why? I told you. Blaire needed my help and I needed the work."

"Well, because of me," he continues, not looking convinced.

"Oh, you? You being here doesn't bother me. I'm—"

"You're over it. I heard." Brody, still in full Santa gear, looks like someone took Rudolph out back and shot him. I don't want to tell him the truth—I'm not sure I'll ever be over it. But I do want to make the distraught look on his face go away.

"So, how does Santa spend a day off away from the North Pole?"

Brody recovers quickly. "There are a few things I need to get —I came up here so suddenly I left some essentials behind." He looks down at his phone and sighs. "And looks like all the cars are busy. Wanted to go tonight, but I guess not. If I wait too much longer, I'm going to fall asleep."

"I'll take you." The words leave my mouth before I can process having formed them.

"You'll take me?"

"You really need to stop repeating what I'm saying," I say, making sure my words have a teasing tone. I remember how seriously Brody can take things.

"Sorry." His cheeks flush red, and I remember something else that attracted me to Brody. His self-assuredness would be potent in its own, but mixed in with his humility and tendency to flush when he's caught off-balance? Christmas kryptonite. "You . . . you know taking me means you'll be alone with me. In the car and in the store."

"Well, I don't think the store will be *that* dead, even at 9:00 p.m. It is the holiday shopping season after all."

"But, you'll take me. You'll take me to the store?" His tone couldn't be more surprised if he tried.

"Yeah, sure." I shrug. "Like I said, I'm—"

"Over it." Another voice cuts in from my left. Like a bubble burst, Brody and I wear matching shocked expressions to find out we're not alone yet. Jimmy smirks my way, his look one that knows too much, before he softens his grin for Brody. "Wanted to check a couple of database things with you before I took off, Mr. Santa. Sound okay?"

Brody looks at me with a question in his eye. If I have time to think about it, will I take back my offer? Maybe I should, but something in me—the self-destructive streak that's always run far and wide in my life—is louder than my sanity. "I'll head back to the school now and get changed. Make sure the Bronco is clean enough for such an important passenger. Plus, I'll warm it up too."

This time the flush reaches the whole way to Brody's earlobes. I'd bet my salary for the next week that the tips of his ears are red under his hat too. I teased him all the time about being from the South and a big baby when it comes to the cold. Maybe after a decade of life in New York City he's finally used to it, but there's something different about a New England chill.

"Sounds good. I'll see you soon. And thanks."

He snaps back into focus mode, looking at the screen Jimmy's holding up for him. I'm almost upset at how easily he's able to brush off the fact that we're about to be truly alone, without the chance of someone interrupting. *Self-destruction dialed up to eleven.* But as I head to the door with a few of the other elves, I feel it—the heat of his gaze on my back. Right before I shut the door firmly behind me, I look back. And this time, when I catch his eyes on me, he doesn't look away.

$$Chapter\ 6$$

Brody

When I walk into the parking lot next to the gymnasium, I'm expecting Austin to be long gone. There's an SUV running in the lot, parking lights on and exhaust puffing a white cloud tinged yellow in the glow of the street lamps around us. Walking closer, I can make out a familiar silhouette in the driver's seat. I take a deep breath and after another few steps, pull up even with the driver's side door. My knock on the window is muffled by the thick fabric of my gloves, but it's still enough to startle Austin. His body jolts and then levels me with a glare clearly meant to say, "What the fuck are you doing on this side of the car?"

"We good?" I say out loud, my hand folding into a thumbs up seemingly outside of my control. I don't miss the eye roll before Austin jerks his head, indicating I should walk around to the other side of the car and get in.

"I thought you might have left," I say, buckling my seat belt and looking over to my left. He busies himself with putting the car in reverse and navigating us out of the parking spot.

"We're going to Wally World, right? And of course I didn't leave. I said I'd take you, and I'm taking you."

There's no bite behind the words, but I hear the underlying

meaning. *I keep my word, unlike someone we both know.* But he's over it.

We ride in uncomfortable silence as Austin navigates us out of downtown Holly Ridge and onto the State Route toward the box store. Wally World technically exists within Winterberry Glen limits, a fact Holly Ridge never forgot in their shop small promotions when I lived here.

"What happened to the feud between Holly Ridge and Winterberry Glen?"

"So, Santa doesn't shop small?" Austin asks his question at the same time I ask mine.

"You first," we both say in unison again, before our chuckles finally slice the tension.

"It ended with the Christmas festival five years ago, really. It's how Blaire and Cole met. Holly Ridge would have lost their town charter and become part of Winterberry Glen if the festival hadn't been so successful that year."

Each passing streetlight allows me a glimpse of Austin's handsome face for a second every few hundred feet. "Cole had the assignment of overseeing Blaire's work. During the planning, they did some digging on the origins of the feud, and from what they learned, Blaire led changes to bring the towns together to plan the holiday festival and helped end some of the bad blood. The week leading up to the football game between the high schools can get pretty ugly, but things are a lot better now."

He'd always been such a good storyteller. I want to ask him to tell me more, just to watch him talk about his hometown and listen to his voice.

"So, why doesn't Santa shop small?" Austin's question breaks me out of my trance, and I'm glad his eyes are on the road, not watching how sappily I've been staring at him.

"The beard and hair coloring is semi-permanent, especially when I'm wearing it daily. Sort of ruins the illusion if you see Santa in the next aisle over, carrying deodorant and condoms, doesn't it?" I curse internally, blaming the Austin-trance for scrambling my brain and using condoms as an example. Toothpaste, toilet paper, hell, even athlete's foot spray. All such better examples to say to your ex than the word condom.

"Ha." Austin's tone goes flat. "I can see your point. Well, I can't promise you won't run into any kids up past their bedtime here, but you can borrow some sunglasses if you need to borrow the tried-and-true, under-the-radar look of the rich and famous. You've already got the hat."

I pulled down on the hunter-green knit beanie self-consciously. Would he remember it as the one he gave me for the one Christmas we spent together? Surely not.

We finish the rest of the ride in silence, and the few moments left of the trip drag out forever. We finally pull into a parking spot and I'm surprised to find myself wanting to get away from Austin. It's depressing to think about, but maybe we're too broken. Maybe we need the buffer of other people for us to spend time together without it feeling like we're forcing down fruitcake. The weeks between now and Christmas stretch out ahead of me at the thought.

"Okay, well, I'll only be a minute."

Austin doesn't answer me, but instead climbs out of the car and waits for me at the back. I scramble to unbuckle myself, having to slow down and carefully open the door so I don't hit the car parked too close, squeezing to fit between Austin's SUV and their door.

Any impatience I expect to find on his face isn't there. Instead, his eyes bounce from me back to the too-close car, like he's recalibrating his expectations. "Sorry, I didn't realize how close they were on your side."

"And my body's a bit more traditional Santa-like than when you saw me last." I chance a glance in his direction as we walk to the door. Austin bites his lip and shoves his hands in his pockets, seeming to use all of his energy not to take the bait I'm dangling. It's fair—questions about the change in my body shape would lead to why I'm not a lawyer anymore, and to why I'm a professional Santa. I want to share it all with Austin. More than anything. But he needs to be ready to hear it.

"So, what all did you say you needed? Deodorant and condoms?" Leave it to Austin to put me right back in the hot seat.

"I don't need . . . I don't even know why I said that. I don't buy condoms that often. Not that I don't use them. Safe sex and all. Not that I have a lot of sex. I mean, some. A normal amount." Sticking my foot further and further into my mouth, I realize Austin isn't beside me anymore. I whirl around, hoping I can blame part of the cherry redness of my cheeks on the bitter cold. He's leaning against a candy cane sleeved bollard in front of the automatic door, laughing his head off. After what seems to be an excessively long laugh break, he straightens up and wipes underneath his eyes.

"Was it really *that* funny?"

"It was pretty funny," he says, walking past me and grabbing a waiting cart. I consider letting him get a head start but quicken my steps to catch up with him. "But, I dunno. You're . . . you're different, Brody. It catches me off guard, and sometimes, makes me laugh." His eyes widen with surprise at admitting so much. He shrugs and tries to play it off as he starts walking toward the pharmacy section.

"You're different too, you know," I say quietly. A hitch in Austin's step is the only indication I get he's heard me.

After I've gathered the essentials I need, and Austin's added his twelve-pack of toilet paper and four-pack of Red Bull to the cart, we head to the checkout. Too late in the day for the self-checkouts to be open, we take our place in line behind a few other groups.

Somewhere between Austin teasing me for sniffing the deodorant I've used since I left for college to be sure it smells the same and being fake-horrified I need to buy more underwear, because it means I didn't pack enough, our silence becomes comfortable, not awkward. We wait in silence now, both exhausted from the day. Well, I'm exhausted. Austin cracked one of his energy drinks halfway through our shopping excursion and is currently bouncing on the balls of his feet.

The bright yellow writing on the cover of one of the magazines lining the checkout aisle catches my eye. "Go old school. Play 20 Questions to rekindle the spark with your man." I'm trying to imagine the look on Austin's face if I suggest we play Twenty Questions on the way home, when his voice breaks through my brain fog.

"Brody." His tone makes it clear it's not the first time he's said my name. "We're next. Wanna start loading the belt?" His toilet paper and Red Bull, with the box open, are already there, waiting for the cashier to move them forward. I shake my head, trying to physically remove the notion of Austin agreeing to rekindle anything with me, and step up to the cart. Austin and I work together to pile everything onto the waiting space, and I'm surprised by how much I grabbed. Maybe I didn't *need* all this tonight, but it'll save me another trip later to have it. And, as exhausted as I am, maybe I didn't want our shopping trip to be over.

"Youse guys together?" the cashier asks as she starts moving the belt toward her.

"No!" I exclaim while Austin responds, "Separate, please" in a much calmer tone. My cheeks start to warm again, but the cashier couldn't care less, shrugging before saying, "Youse shared a carriage and didn't put up a divider. Remember, we were the first state to legalize gay marriage. Just because I could be your grandmother doesn't mean I'm going to assume heteronormative bullshit."

Austin and I exchange a glance, and I bite my lip to keep from giggling. "Thanks for your support, ma'am," Austin says with a straight face while he taps his card to the reader. Progressive grandma starts scanning my things, and Austin swings around to the end to start bagging.

"You've got a real knack for bagging, young man," she says after she reads my total, admiring his handiwork.

Austin shrugs but doesn't deny it. "Stints at Doose's Market in the Glen over the years helped. Besides, we've held up your line enough, so wanted to get out of your hair."

I look at the line behind me, twice as long as when we joined the queue. Guess I'm not the only one who needs a late-night essentials run.

"You boys have a good night now." Our cashier nods at us and turns to the person behind us. "You know, these Styrofoam plates are awful for the environment," she says as she rings up their first item.

A snicker escapes before I can stop it this time, and I push the cart a little too hard. Austin jumps out of the way, so I don't run him over. We both lose it, laughing the whole way through the parking lot.

"She sure was something else, huh?" I say once we're back in the car, waiting for it to warm up. Well, I am—Austin seems immune to the cold. Must be earned after close to four decades of New England winters.

"If you're going to work the overnight shift in retail, you've gotta find your ways to make it fun. There are some real whackadoos who come out at night, even worse during a full moon."

"It was the same at the law firm. No one would want to admit to being superstitious, but anytime a Friday the thirteenth matched up with a full moon, we all held our breath knowing we'd either be in for some wild cases or erratic cold calls."

"I mean, there's definitely a difference between what you'll see working overnight at a service center and working in Manhattan at a high-rise law firm. But sure, I guess I can see your point." Even though the heater is running full tilt, the temperature inside the car drops to frigid level. In an instant, the tentative peace we've found is gone. We need to find a way not to have to tiptoe around the past, but how?

The bright yellow print from the magazine cover comes back to mind. Maybe you don't have to declare you're playing Twenty

Questions to bring about the spirit of the game. I clear my throat and ask, "What did you mean when you said I'm different?"

The question is met with silence as we approach a streetlight turning red. Great, let's drag out this car ride even more, if he's not even going to answer a direct question. I sneak a glance Austin's way to find his smirk on full-blast, aimed right at me.

"Trying to play Twenty Questions to rekindle things with your man?"

Busted.

Chapter 7

Austin

The light turns green, meaning I have to stop watching Brody squirm. I decide to take pity on him and answer. Well, it's not entirely pity. I have some questions of my own.

"Wanting to know *why* you're asking the question is a good place to start. Before Brody, on the path to being a corporate prosecutor, asked all sorts of sharp questions. I felt like you were interviewing me on at least our first three dates. But Santa Brody?" His head whips in my direction, and I wince, realizing it's the first time I've called him that out loud. I push on. "Santa Brody is a little softer. More reserved and more cautious. More aware of the weight his words carry and the impact they can have on someone else."

"Okay . . ." he says, slow and soft. When I sneak another glance, he's looking out the window. Did I get too real with him? I guess maybe this is another way Santa Brody differs from the one I knew—he's more willing to show how other's words affect *him*. "And it's way easier to make you blush now, too."

Brody brings his hands up to his cheeks, forgetting we're in the dark and the flush isn't nearly as visible. "I dunno, you were always pretty good at making me blush."

I lose my mind at a stop sign and look over to throw him a wink. He averts his eyes to look down. My eyes trace over the green knit hat I gave him for Christmas all those year ago—I recognized it right away and am trying not to let knowing he kept it get to me. A passing streetlight lets me get a glimpse of his blush, his lower lip tucked between his teeth. While he's off his guard, I strike.

"Why did you leave ten years ago without saying goodbye? You weren't at UMass. What happened?" Brody looks up, his eyes wide and stricken. Before I can name all the emotions I see flash through them, a car honks its horn behind me. My eyes are forced back on the road. The silence hangs around us like a weight. Will Brody's answer lift it off or pull it down to smother me?

"UMass pulled my funding at the last minute. Columbia and Dartmouth both gave away my spots. *The plan* said I needed to go to law school that year, and I needed to be fully funded. My blinders were on so tight, and I had been following the plan for so long, I couldn't consider any other option. I had to call my grandma for the first time in a decade, tail between my legs to ask her to pull strings at NYU. It's where my grandpa went to law school and they're major donors. NYU found a fully-funded spot for me within a day."

I roll this over in my mind, still not seeing how changing schools leads to leaving a committed relationship without saying goodbye. Well, I guess he wrote it in the note he left me, but I'm not willing to count that.

"Okay . . . so you were going to New York instead of right down the road. We could have made the distance work. I would have come with you?"

"I heard you, you know." The pain in Brody's voice cuts through me. My fingers clutch the steering wheel tighter to keep from reaching for him. "I heard you tell Cole you'd come to Columbia with me, back when we didn't know where I'd end up. You even being in my life contradicted the plan. No serious relationships until after I made partner, no distractions. But, if I went to UMass, I thought I could have both. You would be here and so would I."

"So what, you allowed me to factor into your decision for law schools, and when you lost your funding, you blamed me?" My head is spinning, and I've never been more thankful for the fifteen mile per hour speed limit along the streets of Holly Ridge.

"Yes and no. You *were* the reason I chose UMass, *and* I couldn't let you come with me."

My mouth opens but no words come out. My brain is whirring too fast to stop on a single thought. The leather of the wheel creaks under my hands. My existence screwed up his plan? He couldn't "let me go with him"? Did I embarrass him? My small-town, high school graduate self didn't fit into his perfect vision for his life, so he let me go?

I realize we're in front of Jitters and I still haven't said anything. What is there to say, really?

"Austin?" Brody starts, his voice tentative and nervous. It's trying to reach me across the gap he widened between us with his words, but there's no rope in the world long enough to reach the other side right now.

"Got it. Now I know. Well, I won't burden you with my presence anymore tonight. Your stuff's in the back." I reach down and pull the lever, knowing I'm being a first-class ass, not even helping him unload everything, but even the thought of looking at him hurts.

"Austin, wait. I don't think—"

"Goodnight, Brody," I say, infusing as much finality into my tone as I can muster. My eyes stay trained on the crack in the steering wheel leather. I know he's looking at me, his gaze hot on the side of my face. Eventually, he pops open the door and gets out.

"Goodnight, Austin," he says, right before the door closes. Still, I don't look up, through the closing of the back hatch and the clunking up the steps in his boots. It's quiet enough I hear what might be the door to the studio close. But still, I keep my eyes trained forward, blurry now with tears I will myself not to shed.

After I know there's no chance he's out there watching me, I wipe my eyes and put the Bronco into drive. The deserted roads and a desire to get home as quickly as possible without going the whole way around the square has me execute a three-point turn to go back the way I came. And there, in the rearview mirror, a curtain from above the coffee shop twitches closed.

Chapter 8

Brody

I've dreamed a million times about explaining to Austin what happened when I left. How I regretted it instantly, but still knew I made the right choice to not bring him with me. He belongs in Winterberry Glen. I couldn't be the reason he left the place that needs him.

I'd even imagined it going terribly wrong. But I never imagined him cutting me off and leaving me out in the cold—literally.

I get nothing done on my day off. I'm sure I slept at some point, but when I walk into the locker room thirty-six hours later, it sure doesn't feel like it. But then I see a mop of dark brown, almost black hair, and throw a thank you up to Santa in heaven I timed my arrival perfectly.

"Austin," I say. His eyes meet mine, and the nothingness I see in them stops me short. No anger, no sadness. Barely a hint of recognition. Just nothing.

"Uh, hi." Everything I planned to say flies out of my head.

He nods in response and looks back down at his leggings, straightening out the horizontal lines so they're even.

"Ileftsomethinginyourcar." All one word, not a breath. And to think, I used to argue cases for a living.

"Huh?" At least he speaks to me, even if it's to seek clarity about what a bozo I'm being.

"I left something in your car. It's actually, well, more than one something, so I know I didn't forget to buy it, so I think maybe a bag made it into the back seat? Did you see it?"

He looks somewhere over my left shoulder. "There's a bag behind the driver's seat, but I figured it was trash or something."

"Oh, I bet it's my bag then," I say. My voice carries an inordinate amount more cheer than required for asking about a missing bag of toiletries. "Maybe after the shift we can go grab it?"

Austin turns for his locker and reaches inside. He reaches toward me without really looking at me, and I realize he's handing me his keys.

"I have to leave early today, so why don't you go get it now?"

"You're . . . you're leaving early? But there has to be someone there to help the kids after they see Santa." Again, too much emotion, this time indignation at the idea he'd abandon his post.

"The kids will be fine. I'm going to take over as a greeter for today. I texted with Minh last night. You can put the keys back in my locker. The combination is my birthday." His eyes lock with mine and a bit of angry heat pours into them. "If you didn't decide to leave that behind, too."

All the air leaves me in a big exhale. Getting away from me now and being sure to get away from me in the workshop too. I guess this is my life for the next three-and-a-half-weeks. "I remember. I . . . I make a donation to the Cancer Society every year on your birthday."

This takes Austin so much by surprise he forgets he's supposed to be indifferent. Shock, then raw emotion filter across his face before he gets ahold of himself and leaves behind a blank slate. His mouth opens and closes twice before he turns around and walks out without another word.

I slump against the lockers, exhausted before even working a minute of today's shift. The chai latte with cinnamon Susie made for me grows cold in my hand and curdles in my stomach. I hate thinking this is how the rest of my time in Holly Ridge will be. There has to be something I can do to fix it. I straighten back up and head to Austin's SUV to grab the bag of things he must have put in the back seat when we were unloading the other night. He needs some time. I hope.

The cold air whips against my cheeks as I step out of the gym, and I realize I've forgotten to put my coat back on. I pick up my pace, remembering the weatherman on the news last night predicting an even deeper freeze than already here.

The car beeps as I hit the unlock button, and my hand pauses on the door handle in shock. A car seat sits above where I can see the white handle of the plastic bag resting on the floor. Was it there the other night? Surely, I would have noticed something of that size. I try to remember, but all that comes are flashes of Austin's gorgeous face in the dim, usually unflattering light and the hurt I put there before he told me to go.

Does Austin have a *kid*?

I go through the motions of retrieving my bag and head back inside to get changed. Potentially life-rearranging news isn't an excuse to keep any eager Santa visitors waiting.

As I put on the velvet red suit, my mind turns over what it might mean if Austin does have a kid. Austin would be a great dad. Yanking my hat into place, I realize other than the fact he might be in a relationship with the child's mother, it doesn't change anything. *Especially because right now he's not talking to you or even looking at you.* I wince at the honesty of my inner voice. Yeah, there's that whole barrier too.

I put my coat back on and beat a quick path over to the workshop. Stomping snow off my boots, I realize just how close I cut my arrival today. My eyes immediately search out Austin as I sit down in the Santa chair and snag onto his back where he stands talking to one of the other elves by the front door. Guess he really did ask to switch assignments. Is it only because he's leaving early today? Or will he try to make it permanent, keeping himself far away from me?

"Ready, Santa?" Minh, the switched elf in question asks with a kind smile on his face. Time to stop my moping and get into character.

I put on what I hope is my jolliest smile and nod. "Let's make some magic." Austin pulls open the front door, and it's go time.

We're on our break around six when I see Austin getting his coat on. "I have to go grab Cassidy from her grandma's and take her home. Melody came down with something on the way home from Springfield yesterday." The elf he's talking to has their back to me, so I can't hear their response. Austin must feel my gaze because his eyes shoot to mine, locking for a quick second, before he looks away. "Yeah, well, anything I can do to help, you know? Have a good evening, Monty. I'll see you all tomorrow."

A moment later, Austin's out the door, and I'm left staring behind him.

"So, what happened with you and Mr. Austin?" I jump slightly, finding Jimmy standing next to me.

"You sneak up on everyone like that?" I say, hoping to avoid his question.

He shrugs. "It happens more often than you think. So, what happened with you and Mr. Austin? At the beginning of the week, it was all tense, but in like a hot way. Now, it's all tense, but in a sad way."

I blink at the kid, a little dumbfounded he picked up on any energy between us at all, let alone the change. "Does everyone . . ." I trail off, too embarrassed to finish my sentence.

Jimmy shakes his head. "Nah, just me. Like I told Mr. Austin on Tuesday, it's part of what makes me so good at this. I can read people."

I nod and decide there's really no use in denying it, especially if he's mentioned something to Austin too. Jimmy's from Winterberry Glen; maybe he knows something about Austin's life I don't know.

"So, it sounded like Austin needed to leave early to pick someone up?" I try to sound innocent and nonchalant, but the look on Jimmy's face tells me how badly I failed.

"Like I told him, you need to ask. Even if I knew—which this time I do—I'm not going to tell you."

"You told him to ask me something?"

Jimmy rolls his eyes, and I get the vibe telling grown men how to deal with their feelings is not what he signed on for. "Yeah, he asked me if I knew why you weren't a lawyer anymore. Is that what you talked about to make the vibes all sad between you two?"

"Uh, no," I say. "He asked why I left ten years ago without saying goodbye. I think I did a really bad job explaining it, since you know, now he won't talk to me."

"You just packed up and left?" Jimmy asks. "Damn Santa, that's cold."

Even though he's calling me out on my terrible decision-making and even more terrible emotion handling, my lips curl up in a smile. "It's not Mister Santa then?"

Jimmy shakes his head. "Nah, I think we're on a first name basis now."

"So, are you going to tell me what to do next?"

He shakes his head. "I think you know what you need to do. Now you gotta figure out how to make it happen. So, if you're done being all sad, now that Mr. Austin is gone, do you want to take a look at the database I built after we close up tonight?"

I can't help but laugh at the abrupt subject change. "Yeah, sure. I'm sorry I wasn't here early enough to do it before. We can head to Jitters, and I'll buy you a drink?" His eyes widen. "A hot cocoa-type drink—Santa can't buy his elf a beer, even if he may or may not be of age."

Chapter 9

Austin

I pull into Cole and Blaire's driveway, leaving the engine idling while I take a deep breath. After feeling suffocated by the day with Brody, I'm happy I had an excuse to bail out a little early today. It's not the time to dwell on it though. With precious cargo in the back seat, it's too cold not to get out of the car immediately once the heat is off. Even with the dramatics of Melody throwing up in their minivan on the way home from photos in Springfield yesterday, all while Blaire is away from the girls overnight for the first time, my mind can't stop replaying Brody saying, "I couldn't let you come with me" over and over again.

Cassidy coos in the backseat, bringing me back to the present. "All right, little miss. Let's get you inside to Daddy and see how he and your sister have fared today after your day with Grandma." We hustle through the cold to the front door, which opens for us as we hit the porch.

"Get in, get in, it's freezing," my best friend says, like he's not the one who hasn't left the house all day.

"Oh really? I hadn't noticed." My snark dies on my lips as I take in the state of the living room behind Cole. "Melody didn't suddenly learn how to walk, did she?"

Cole rakes his hand through his hair. "No, but this is the first time all day she's let me put her down and stayed asleep. Her fever finally broke, so I think she's feeling better." He reaches for Cassidy, and I hand her over, using my free hands to start picking up bottles and burp cloths.

"Hi, baby. Daddy missed you." I turn, ready to snark I missed him too, but the sight of Cole looking at his daughter with so much joy makes the words freeze in my throat. I can't help but wonder when the last time was I looked that happy.

Cole follows me into the kitchen, where I toss the burp cloths toward the door to the laundry and drop the bottles in the sink. I pull open the dishwasher to find it full of clean dishes and get to work putting them away.

"You know, this is becoming a bad habit of yours, making yourself at home," he says, bouncing Cassidy on his arm, a smirk on his face.

"Consider it back pay for all the times you helped us out," I say, not needing to look back at Cole to know his expression had changed to one of pity.

"That's different. Your mom was sick, and you were working three jobs to keep you guys afloat. Doing some dishes and running the vacuum while you were out at treatments is the least I could do."

"I know," I say, putting away the last bowl and starting to rinse what's in the sink to load the dishwasher again. "And now, you've got *your* hands full. I know you and Blaire are doing better than floating, but I can help, so I will." Cole steps up next to me at the counter, and I finally look his way.

"What's brought this up? Is everything okay?" His face is full of concern, his voice soft and full of care.

"Oh, she's fine. She had her scans last month, and everything is still clear. I dunno, your life is so different now, and this is a way I can still fit."

Cole's expression turns to one of shock, his mouth open. "Of course you still fit, Austin. There's a reason we didn't even consider anyone else to be the girls' godfather. You don't have to earn your place in our life. We love having you around."

Emotion catches in my throat for the second time since I walked through the front door. I'm not afraid to express my emotions, but I haven't cried in months, and now twice in almost as many days? Fucking Brody.

My best friend's eyes widen with understanding. "Do you want to grab these girls a bottle and sit by the fire?"

"And I thought I didn't need to earn my place," I tease, knowing exactly what Cole is trying to do.

"I can certainly try to feed them both at once, but I think you'd rather have a cute baby to focus on while you tell me what happened with Brody." He hands me Cassidy without another word and heads to grab Melody from her bassinet in the living room.

"Your daddy thinks he knows everything," I say to the happy girl in my arms, grabbing one of the formula mixed bottles. We're settled into my usual armchair, slurping away when Cole comes in with a much happier looking baby than the last time I saw her. The fact that she's not covered in sour-smelling formula vomit helps too.

"So, what happened after the store Tuesday night?"

I look at him wide-eyed, wondering how he knows about our late-night activities. I feigned a headache on the drive yesterday to avoid any questions about my sullen mood, and Melody's exorcist impression on the way home distracted us the rest of the way.

He scoffs at me. "C'mon, your cashier was Barbara, and she recognized our new Santa. She referred to you as a mystery man when she told Susie about it, but I knew exactly who the Superman lookalike she referred to was. So, what happened?"

I roll my eyes at the gossip train in these towns, but let out a deep sigh and start talking nonetheless. "Things were okay. Awkward, sure, but we started to turn the corner. And then he wanted to play Twenty Questions. Don't ask," I say in response to

Cole's confused look. "So I asked him why he left without saying goodbye or telling me he wasn't going to UMass."

Cole whistles. "No easing him into it there, huh?"

I shrug, and Cassidy shoots me an annoyed look before going back to finishing her bottle. "I blame the 10:00 p.m. Red Bull. And the fact wondering has plagued me for the last decade."

He nods in understanding. "So what did he say?"

I take a deep breath, preparing myself to say out loud the words that cut me so deeply. "He told me I'm the reason he decided to go to UMass. He heard me tell you I'd go with him to Columbia, so when he ended up needing to change course and go to NYU, he couldn't let me go with him. Guess I didn't measure up to the type of boyfriend you introduced to fellow corporate lawyers or something."

Cole blinks at me. "He couldn't let you? Or he didn't want you to?"

"He couldn't let me." I look back down at the now-sleeping baby in my arms, trying to let the love I feel for her wash out the hurt and shame threatening to drown me at the idea of once again not being good enough.

"And then what did he say?"

"What do you mean?"

"Did he elaborate any on why he couldn't let you?"

"No, I think it was pretty clear."

Cole's face takes on the look you give a child when they throw a tantrum over something unreasonable. "I don't think it's clear at all. Leaving you without saying goodbye notwithstanding, Brody's not a cruel person, Austin. And he loved you a whole fucking lot."

I huff out a breath. "I don't know that you can discount one of the cruelest things you can do to a person you supposedly love. If he fucking loved me so much, how could he just leave?"

"Or did he love you so fucking much he felt he had no choice but to leave like that?"

I tilt my head to rest on the back of the chair, turning over

Cole's question in my mind, wondering if he's right. Did Brody's explanation have more to it I didn't give him time to share before I kicked him out of my car? Why didn't he make me listen?

I break the silence after a few minutes. "At some point, we're going to have to start watching our language, or their first word is going to be one that Blaire will fucking kill us for."

We both laugh, breaking the heavy feeling hovering over the room.

"You know you need to talk to him again. When you're ready."

I nod. "Yeah, when I'm ready." But can you ever be ready to give someone the chance to break your heart again?

The next two days don't find me in a ready state of mind. I keep my role switched with Minh, stationing me by the front door. Facing a blast of arctic air every few minutes feels more appealing than having to look into Brody's sad eyes after every child hops off his lap. And this air is extra frigid—the polar vortex the weather people kept predicting is firmly swirling around us. Blaire's best friend, Charlotte, who I claim as one of my best friends too, sent me a video this morning. Her future sister-in-law is a meteorologist in Washington, DC, and has an online video explaining what they mean by polar vortex. The center of this one seems to be right over Holly Ridge and Winterberry Glen.

Soon enough, the first Saturday of my short career as an elf is winding down. We had to force Brody to take his breaks. He wants to get through as many kids as possible. But no one wants to be responsible for scarring children because Santa passes out from dehydration or lack of food.

The door shuts behind the last family at 5:30, thirty minutes later than we're supposed to close, but Santa Brody won't let anyone feel rushed. I want to be annoyed with him, but I can't be.

Even when I'm mad or hurt or whatever emotions I feel toward him at any moment, I still have to admire how good he is at this.

We're resetting everything for tomorrow when there's a sudden pounding at the back door.

"Think that's a kid trying to see Santa to tell him his family disappeared?" I joke.

Minh gets my Home Alone reference right away. "I think this Santa would ask a few more questions and call CPS or something."

Someone must have answered the door while we were yapping, and suddenly Susie is in Santa's Workshop, looking flustered. I hope something didn't happen to the big delivery she's supposed to get for the sugar cookie decorating event tomorrow. Blaire worried the trucks wouldn't be able to start in the cold.

"We . . . we have a problem," she says looking at Brody. Shit, it is the delivery. Susie knows Brody isn't really Santa, right? He can't send reindeer to go fly and pick up the supplies?

"What's up, Susie?" Brody asks. "Is everything okay?"

"No. Well, yes. No one's hurt, but the pipes in the crawl space above the studio apartment burst." Everyone's stopped what they're doing by now to listen, and a unified gasp emits from at least half of us. "Jitters is okay. There are some wet supplies and boxes. We're able to keep the water on for the shop and turn it off to the apartment, but the unit flooded before we got it shut off. Brody, I'm so sorry, but you're not going to be able to stay there."

"It's okay, Susie. These things happen when it gets so cold. I'm sure there's a hotel—"

Jasmine cuts him off. "No way, especially not on the first festival weekend in December. Everything within thirty miles has been booked since June."

Brody's face falls. It does something to me to see Santa look so lost. The fact that it's Santa Brody is even worse. The urge to offer to take him in rises, but I try to tamp it down. He stomped all over my heart *again* a few days ago. I cannot bring him into my space.

"Austin, don't you have a spare room?" I look around, bewildered, wondering if my subconscious grew its own voice. I find Jimmy standing to my right, looking smug.

"Oh, Jimmy, great idea," Susie says, giving Brody a meaningful look. "I know you were *friends* when Brody lived here before."

Somehow, I'm the one who's blushing now, everyone looking my way. Well, everyone except Brody. He's looking at the floor, like he expects me to say no.

"Yeah, sure, I do have a spare room," I say, my eyes on Brody so our gazes meet when he lifts his head.

"Oh wonderful." Susie claps her hands, and that's enough to break the spell over everyone, setting them into motion to get out of here and get home—probably to check on their own pipes.

I turn to Jimmy, who looks very pleased with himself at what's happened here. "I thought you said nobody else knew?"

He has the balls to look innocent. "I said everyone didn't know. I didn't say no one knew. It's Susie. Susie knows everything." He has me there.

Jimmy claps a hand on my shoulder and heads back to his post to shut down the computer for the night. I walk my way over to where Brody and Susie are talking.

" . . . run up and grab a few things, there's still a laundromat in Winterberry Glen where I can wash stuff, right?"

An indignant noise escapes before I can stop it. "You can use my laundry if you're staying with me, Brody. I'm not a monster."

This causes Brody's cheeks to redden, and he looks busted. "I don't want to put you out more than me staying with you already does."

Susie's eyes bounce between us trying to read the vibe, and the delighted look on her face doesn't match the news she delivers next. "In any case, the water ran out under the door to the apartment and down the steps. It's a hazard for anyone who's not a hired contractor to go up there until it gets fixed up. My insurance broker would have my head if they knew I let you on those ice-covered stairs. I'm sure Austin can lend you something."

My breath hitches, imagining Brody wearing my clothes, wearing nothing at all. *Nope, we're not going there. You're letting him stay because otherwise you would have looked like an ass in front of everyone you worked with, and one of the core gossip cogs in these towns. There's no other reason.*

"Yeah, I'm sure we can figure something out." I try to keep my tone even, as the reality that Brody, the person I've tried to keep out of my head and out of my life for the past ten years, is soon going to be in my home sinks in.

What could possibly go wrong?

Chapter 10

Brody

The ride over to Winterberry Glen and Austin's house is silent. I know small towns are known for their scheming, but forcing Austin to take me in really feels like a bridge too far. My mouth lifts in a smile as we literally cross the bridge while I have that thought.

"You know, we can call some hotels. I'm sure someone, somewhere, has a room. You didn't have to say yes."

"You play Santa, not Jesus. I don't think you understand how big of a deal this festival has become, even more so over the past few years. Now with the expansion, so activities take place in both towns, the area hosts even more people. Those hotels have waiting lists double-digit names deep."

I exhale deeply as we crawl down Main Street of Winterberry Glen. The trees lining the streets are strung with lights, each lamppost home to a colorful holiday design, and the sidewalks teeming with people. He's right—this is way bigger than the festival we went to all those years ago.

"Okay, well still, if—"

"I'm a big boy, Brody. I can say no if I need to, and I didn't, so just drop it, okay?" His voice is sharp, like there's nothing more in the world he wants than to stop having this conversation.

We fall back into our uneasy silence. Austin finally turns off the main road, and squeezes into a resident-only parking spot along the sidewalk.

"Parking is hell. Visitors don't really seem to care about resident-only signs, and the city doesn't want to put off tourists by towing or giving tickets. We got lucky this time."

I know he's trying to make peace, but I don't have anything to contribute that doesn't sound absolutely asinine in my head, so I keep my mouth shut. I snag the garment bag holding my suit and follow Austin to the front door of a small apartment building.

He looks down at the bag in my hand, and his face takes on a look of worry. "Oh shit, your suits. Are they going to be okay?"

I can't help but smile at the honesty in his concern. "I keep them in checked-bag caliber garment bags even when they're in my closet in case of emergencies like this one. They'll probably need a trip to the dry cleaner because of all the moisture once we can get in, but as long as it's only a few days, it should be fine."

Austin unlocks the front door, nodding in satisfaction with my answer, and leads me inside. "I did see temperatures are supposed to be back in the teens by the beginning of the week. Hopefully, warmer days and direct sunlight are enough to melt the ice on the steps."

We head up one level to the second floor, and Austin unlocks the door to Unit 203. I'm hit with the smell of vanilla and spice—pure Austin—as soon as we walk into his apartment. It's going to be hell staying here, especially if he refuses to talk about the other night.

"Sorry it's such a mess," he says, scrambling to grab plates and scattered mail. "I wasn't expecting company this weekend." I watch as he heads to the kitchen to drop off his armload. Hell, and yet, I don't want to be anywhere else.

"Your room is down the hall, second door on the left," he yells over the water running in the sink. "I'll be back in a second to find you something to sleep in."

I look around, taking in his place as I slowly move to follow his directions to the room I'll be staying in. I'm struck by the lack of toys or anything to indicate Austin's kid spends any time here. I forgot to check for a car seat, so focused instead on not vibrating apart that Austin and I were going home to the same place. Maybe he and the mom aren't together?

The hallway I walk down only has three doors. One for Austin's room, one for the bathroom, and one for this spare room. I turn into the room he indicated and find a cushy armchair, a desk, and some bookshelves covered in photos and knickknacks. I stand in the doorway, confused. Not only is there not a place for a child to sleep, but there's also not a bed for an adult to sleep in. Surely he doesn't expect . . .

"Why are you in the doorway?" Austin steps up behind me, able to see over my shoulder with his few extra inches of height. "Oh, right. I'll need to grab some sheets and . . ."

"Do you have a kid?" I blurt out at the same time he finishes his sentence, "Make up the pullout."

"Wait, what?" I turn around to face him. "Why do you think I have a kid?"

My face heats. "When I got the stuff out of your Bronco the other day, you had a car seat in the back. And then you told Marty you had to leave early to pick someone up from grandma's so . . ."

Understanding dawns on his face. "Oh, no. I mean, yes, there was a car seat, but only so I could go get one of Cole and Blaire's twins from her parents' house. Blaire is out of town and one of the girls was sick, so they took Cassidy to Blaire's mom for the day. Her parents had tickets for a show or something, so I volunteered to go grab her so Cole didn't have to leave the house."

"Oh. That's really nice of you," I finish. Calling it nice seems inadequate, but it's all I can manage as I recalibrate. He doesn't have a kid.

"He's my best friend. Well, they both are. There's nothing

more to it," he says matter-of-factly. "I'll go grab some sheets and we'll get the chair pulled out. The base slides out, so it's pretty firm and comfortable, no sharp springs or flimsy mattress." He turns to go get bedding.

I make my way further into the room and over to the bookshelves, wanting to take a closer look at what means so much to Austin he would want to display it. I expect the pictures of Cole and Blaire and ones of his mom. Pictures with people I don't recognize—people who entered his life after I left it.

And then there are the other photos. Photos of Austin dressed as a Pilgrim to help out at a Thanksgiving food drive. Holding up the finish line tape at the county marathon, on the same Main Street we just drove down. Dressed as a scarecrow with his arms around two other people wearing big grins and Sullivan's Farm T-shirts, the sky cornflower blue in the background.

I keep looking and see the paper clippings, the plaques for outstanding service or recognition of achievement. All from things he's done to make his community and the town he lives in better.

He comes back into the room behind me, and I hear the squeak of the chair as he pulls it out to make a bed. I take the coward's way out, not turning around before I speak, but right here in front of me demonstrates what I so royally screwed up last night.

"This. This is why I couldn't let you come with me to New York," I say, my voice thick with emotion. He's silent and still for a while, his movements halted.

"What is?" His tone is wary, like he's not sure he wants to know the answer. And suddenly, I have to turn around. I have to look at him.

I do and gesture to the shelves now behind me. "You are this town, Austin. You've worked in every business on Main Street, are a key link in the phone tree, and are the first person every old lady calls to clean their gutters, fix a light bulb, or change a smoke detector. And now what you've done with the festival and bringing the towns together? I needed to go, but I couldn't be the *only* reason you left too."

He swallows, and I watch it travel down his throat. "But what if I wanted to be more than this town? What if I wanted to be there for you, see what we could be together?"

I shake my head. "You needed to want that for you. Not because of me. I wouldn't have been able to live with myself if I had taken you away from this town, the people who needed you, just because I didn't want to lose you. So, I left." Emotion clogs my voice, and my vision of Austin, white as a ghost, blurs with unshed tears in my eyes.

He clears his throat. "I, uh, I have to go check something."

And this time, he's the one to walk away without looking back.

Chapter 11

Austin

Fucking Cole and his tendency to be right all the fucking time.

I wipe tears from under my eyes, hiding in my room. Hearing Brody describe me, the way he sees me. Or at least saw me. No one's ever framed me in such a positive light. I'm not the guy who can't decide what he wants to do or can't hold a job. Instead, to him, I'm the one who will do whatever the next need is. Go wherever someone needs me.

I think back to the first time I met Brody. He came to Winterberry Glen in the first place to work as a paralegal at Johnsons and Sons. They ordered lunch from the deli I worked at back then. His piercing blue eyes. His shy smile and tendency to blush. Holding himself with confidence among his coworkers, but kind in his interactions at the same time.

Pretty sure he was into men but not wanting to out him as the new guy in town, I hinted, but let him take the lead. Suddenly, I ran into Brody everywhere. At the gym before work, at the town hall for Bingo Night with Mrs. Krazinski, who he rented a room from, in the grocery store. The checkout aisle is where he finally took me up on my weeks of hinting and asked me out, flushing red the whole time.

Johnsons and Sons specializes in Mergers and Acquisitions and flew under the radar despite its strong reputation having its roots in a small town like Winterberry Glen. Brody tried to explain it to me on our first date. Even though I worked hard to get him to ask me out, I was nervous to be on a date with someone as hot and smart as he was. Realizing he had forgotten I'd lived in this town my entire life and gave him the opening for his explanation by asking if he was particularly interested in M&A, it endeared me to him right away knowing he was nervous too.

Shaking myself free from memory lane, I realize I've been away for a while, and it's time to be a grownup and go face my ex. I busy myself finding clothes for Brody to change in to. I'm taller than he is, so even though our body shapes differ, I'm able to find a pair of sweatpants, a T-shirt, and a sweatshirt that should fit him without a problem. My movements stop after I open my drawer of boxer briefs and realize this area might not work for us to share. I snag a Christmas-themed pair, deciding I'll let him make that call and carry the stack of clothes across the hall to his room.

Except Brody's not in his room. The bed is the rest of the way made—*great job hosting, Austin.* I set the clothes on the bed and hurry back toward the living area. Surely I would have heard the front door open if he had left.

When I round the corner to the kitchen, I find him with the fridge door open, wearing the look of someone who got caught with their hand in the cookie jar.

"Sorry, I didn't plan to actually touch anything. I thought I might see what you had in the way of making dinner."

"You can cook?" I ask. "Sorry," I wince. "I didn't mean to sound quite so surprised. When you were here before, you lived on—"

"Protein shakes and chicken and rice. I know." He straightens up and looks me right in the eye. "I have a lot more time to myself to cook now and"—he pats his stomach—"a better and healthier relationship with food, too. So, yes. I can cook."

Wanting to ask why he's not a lawyer, knowing his career change is why he has so much more time chokes me. It wants to come right out of my mouth. Brody smiles a knowing smile and holds up his hand.

"I know. You want to know why I have more time to cook. I want to tell you. I *need* to tell you. But maybe only one life-altering story per night?"

In all my focus on getting him some clothes and panic when I didn't see him in his room, the bomb he dropped barely fifteen minutes ago faded away. It pulses back now, but I'm able to ignore it in the name of food.

"What did you find in the way of dinner?" I ask, walking across the kitchen and opening a cabinet drawer preemptively, knowing what he'll say.

"A whole lot of nothing. Half a jar of pasta sauce, maybe?" he says, but his voice is without judgment. I set another jar of pasta sauce and a box of pasta on the counter.

"Sounds like pasta for dinner then." I smile, and Brody matches it. I know we need to talk about what he revealed, but we can do that with full stomachs. "There're some meatballs in the freezer. I'll get them going too. I put some clothes on your bed if you want. I can throw anything you might need to wear again tomorrow in the wash. We can place a pickup order to grab on the way home tomorrow night for anything you might need in the interim."

I see Brody's eyes widen when I refer to my place as home. An honest slip of the tongue. But even though he decided our future without me ten years ago, I can't deny there's something about having him in my space, getting the chance to know this new and different Brody. It doesn't mean I have to give him my heart. But it might mean I can gain back a friend.

"I'll go get changed then," he says, heading back down the hall. I busy myself with putting water on to boil and preheating the oven. I move the load of towels I left in the dryer two days ago to the waiting hamper, so glad I didn't forget a load in the washer that needs to be rewashed.

Brody shuffles back out into the kitchen, the jeans and sweater he wore all day in hand. I catch a flash of white for his undershirt and black for his boxer briefs in the mix. My eyes flash toward his crotch all on their own. Is he free-balling it in my sweatpants right now? Why does the idea he is *do* something to me?

He's still standing there, clothes in hand. I jolt into action.

"Oh, right. Washer's over here." I walk the five steps across the room to where the stainless-steel stacked unit gleams. Right, I'm sure he spotted it. I open the door, and he tosses his clothes in.

"Did you want to put anything in too, so we're not running a load for six pieces of clothing?" My brain tries to figure out what the other two pieces are while Brody keeps talking. "And if I could bother you for a pair of socks too, that would be great. Floor's a little cold."

His toes lift and fall in order against the linoleum that requires me to keep my feet in slippers even in the heat of summer.

"Oh shit, of course. I'll be right back." I, once again, hurry away from Brody. Finding my back-up slippers in my closet, I grab those, a pair of socks, and the top few things from my hamper. When I make it back to the kitchen, Brody's pouring pasta into the boiling water.

"Here you go." I try to hand him only the slippers and socks, but everything else falls out of my hands too. And there, on the floor, are a pair of Jack-o'-lantern briefs, lying right next to my Turkey Day briefs.

I duck down to grab them. "Swear I've done laundry since Halloween. Since Thanksgiving too, honestly. Sometimes I just grab whatever's on top."

"I didn't say anything." Brody's smile says plenty with the same twinkle in his eye that looks so in place when he's wearing his Santa suit. He leans against the counter and pulls on the wool socks I brought him before stuffing his shoes into the slippers. I busy myself with throwing the rest of my laundry—and shame—into the washer and starting the load.

"So, you have more than one pair of slippers?" Brody asks.

"Yeah," I say, heading to the oven to check on the meatballs. "My mom gets me a pair every year for Christmas, and I usually keep last year's pair in reserve in case I have someone over." How that sounds registers once it's out of my mouth, but it's too late now. Might as well lean into it. "You know what they say—we bisexuals can't keep it in our pants."

"Stop it." The fierceness in Brody's voice makes me turn around to face him. "Stop putting yourself in the slutty bisexual box. Society does it enough for you. You can sleep with whoever you want—it doesn't matter that they may not all share the same parts."

"I . . . I know. I was kidding," I say, my chest warming at the vigor with which Brody defended me.

"Good," he says, nodding once. "Besides, I remember how upset biphobia gets you."

My grin widens, remembering the rant Brody's referring to. Some social media post or another set me off, and I spent a good five minutes ranting about society discounting bisexuals, especially bisexual men. He nodded and listened the whole time. When I finally ran out of steam, he showed me just how much he appreciated my bisexuality by getting on his knees and—

Briiiing.

The oven timer interrupts the sexy memory. One glance at Brody's face, catching the way his eyes dart back up from my crotch, tells me his mind went to the exact same place. Not dangerous at all.

"Time to eat!" I say, my voice too loud. Brody strains the pasta and guesses the cupboard with the bowls right on the first try while I take the meatballs out and warm up some sauce. We're both settled on the couch eating in silence before Brody speaks again.

"You mentioned your mom buys you slippers. How is she doing?"

Brody's time in town came right after Mom's got the "no evidence of disease" news from her doctors. She wanted—no, needed—to get back to some semblance of normal, but I struggled with doing the same. Brody served as a great distraction, but never complained about me having dinner with her a few times a week.

"She's doing great. Had scans a few weeks ago, and they came back clear. She should be retiring from the craft store soon, but is hoping to go part time instead. Says she missed helping people make their visions come to life most of all when she was sick. She's slowed down some with age but will deny it if you suggest that's the case." Our forks clink against the bowls as I work up the nerve to ask what's on my mind. "Do you really make a donation every year on my birthday?"

Brody nods. "Your mom is the most important person in your life, and like I said, one of the reasons I couldn't be the only reason you left Winterberry Glen. I thought a donation was the least I could do. They were small during law school, but have become more sizable since."

It's rude to ask how sizable. But again, the question of why Brody's not a lawyer anymore, and how much money he can possibly make as a professional Santa are at the front of my mind. Brody asked me not to bring it up tonight, so I pivot to the other elephant in the room.

"I know you think you had my best interests at heart in not wanting me to leave the Glen, but you decided it all on your own. That's not fair to me."

Brody nods. "I know. I swear to you, that's the reason I had in my head when I snuck away in the middle of the night. But with some time, and some therapy, I've come to realize how selfish I was to make that decision for you, not selfless like I thought. You weren't part of the plan, and where I was in life, I couldn't see anything outside of the plan. It sounds stupid and small-minded now. For what it's worth, you would have hated Law School Brody. I had to work hard to become a Brody who even deserves to give you an apology."

His eyes never leave mine while he's talking. He holds my gaze even now, but I can see in the tight way he's clutching onto the bowl and grabbing the fabric of his pants he's dying to look away. I hold him in place just a bit longer.

"When I found out you were gone and then found out you had canceled the lease in Amherst, it broke something in me." I try never to think about my drive to the place we toured together, sneaking into the building and knocking on the door, only to have someone else answer. Their moving boxes in various states of unpacked in the background. Cole stayed on the phone with me the whole way home to make sure I made it back safely. "I deleted your number, blocked you on social media, and tried to pretend you never existed. Well, as much as you can pretend someone who's altered you completely doesn't exist."

His eyes break away then. I nudge my knee against his to get them back. "But thank you. For coming back and telling me. I didn't realize how much I needed to hear it. To hear it wasn't me."

A look of understanding dawns on Brody's face. "When I said I couldn't let you come with me, you heard I didn't want you to."

"Yeah, someone else pointed out me cutting you off and not letting you get another word out may have meant I missed some important context. Annoying he was right."

Brody laughs. "Well, at least you listen to Cole."

"Most of the time." I shrug and laugh along with him.

Brody yawns, and I realize it's somehow close to nine. "We better get you off to bed, Santa. We've gotta be back at the work-shop in fewer hours than I want to calculate." I push off the couch and reach my hand out for his dish. "I'll clean up; you hit the bathroom first. There should be a new toothbrush under the sink."

I force myself to take my time cleaning up, not wanting Brody to feel rushed, but also not wanting to be standing there like a creep when he exits. Instead, I time it perfectly so he's walking toward his room as I start down the hall.

"Night, Austin," he says, stretching his arms above his head so a sliver of his back comes visible above his sweatpants.

"Wait," I say, and he turns, alarm in his eyes. "Sorry," I continue. "That sounded more urgent than I meant it to. But you got to ask your question for the night. Now it's my turn." The alarm turns to wary, but he gamely stands there and waits. I realize I don't have a question in mind and scramble to come up with one. Brody absentmindedly scratches the bottom of his stomach, the shirt riding up in the front this time. A trail of hair disappears below the waistband of *my* pants on his lower half, and I have it.

"Tell me," I raise an eyebrow and lower my voice, "are you wearing my gingerbread man underwear?"

Brody's face takes on a wicked look, and he takes two steps backward so he's in the doorway of his room. "No," he says simply before shutting the door in my face.

I'm distracted getting ready for bed, trying desperately not to allow myself to think about Brody's dick in my pants and failing. There's no one to blame for this but myself. I had to go there.

The floorboard creaks like it always does when I cross the threshold into my room. "Night, Austin," sounds through the closed wood, the tone delivering the greeting chock full of pride and mirth this time around.

"Night, Brody," I answer, closing the door behind me with a smile on my face. A smile that remains when I fall asleep almost as soon as my head hits the pillow, faster than I have in years.

Chapter 12

Brody

Any worries I have about sharing space with Austin—well they are probably warranted. In hindsight, getting through a full conversation about why I left the way I did was the easy part.

What I haven't worried enough about are things like how it would feel to see him sleepy-eyed and bed-headed, walking to the bathroom in the morning. Or the joy it brings me to see him so excited to order a new holiday beverage for me at Jitters before our next stint as Santa and elf. The impact of getting to know this older and wiser Austin.

We fall into a pattern of asking one question each night. Sunday, it happens when we're on our way to pick up my curbside order of essentials. Highest on the list is underwear, because I cannot spend another night of Austin shooting not-so-covert glances at my crotch or another morning worried he'll call me out of bed for breakfast before the dark spot where my dick leaked in his pants overnight dries.

"When you go out on a first date," he asks, "what appetizer do you order?" I think for a moment, unsure if I should admit it's been a long time since I've been on a date.

"I'd have to go with an appetizer platter, if they have one.

That way there's a little bit of everything and gives me more of a chance I got their favorite."

"You wouldn't ask them what they wanted instead of taking a guess?" He bites into the granola bar he grabbed from the snack table in the gym when we changed.

"Nah, this way I look decisive. The truth is I really can't pick one option I want for myself, but they benefit too."

After we pick up my order, I ask my question. "If you could be any animal, what animal would you be?"

"An otter, definitely," he answers, needing no time to consider at all.

"Why an otter?" He lets my bonus question slide.

"They eat several times a day, get to hang out and float in the water, and they're just so cute."

"Well, nothing to argue with there," I say, and we lapse into a comfortable silence.

"C'mon Santa, let's get you home," Austin says, turning onto the bridge to cross into Winterberry Glen.

Monday, the questions come earlier, while we're walking back to the gym from Santa's Workshop.

"If you could live anywhere in the world, where would it be?" Austin asks, our shoes crunching the packed snow made extra hard by the still freezing temperatures. Tomorrow is supposed to get into the twenties, and I can hardly wait.

"A town the size of Winterberry Glen, but in a climate like San Francisco. Somewhere it's not as hot in the summer as it is in the South where I grew up, but it's not as balls cold as it is here right now," I say, a shiver racking through my body.

"You wouldn't live in a city? After all your time in New York?"

I decide to give him a hint into what my life has been for the last three years. "I actually moved to Stamford three years ago. I don't need to be in the city every day, so living there gives me a close enough commute, but also got me out of gridlocked Manhattan."

I watch Austin absorb this information, his eyebrows moving up and down slightly, his lips rolling in and out of his mouth. He's building a new Brody in his mind.

A few minutes later we're changing and I decide to ask the same question. "How about you? Where would you live?"

Austin pulls on his sweatshirt before he answers, his head popping out of the neck hole with his hair deliciously ruffled. "I know you can't picture me anywhere but here, but sometimes, I do wonder what it would be like to live in a city. Public transportation, more than a drive-through or pizza place open past eleven. I don't know I could do it forever, but it might be nice to quicken up the pace."

I bend down to tie my shoes, giving myself a few extra beats to answer. "You fit here and play a role in what makes this town so great. Doesn't mean you couldn't fit somewhere else too."

He's looking at me, expression guarded, like he's not sure he should believe me or not. "Somewhere with a community but isn't quite so small town. That's where I see you," I say, satisfied I'm correct in my assessment.

"Say, would that be somewhere like Stamford?" he asks, a shit-eating grin on his face.

I flush. "Sure, Stamford may come close to fitting the bill." I lock down my racing mind feeding me images of us sharing a community, a home. He's teasing, and that's not anywhere close to what he's thinking.

"C'mon, let's go. The chicken you put in the crock pot before we left is calling my name." He holds open the locker room door so I can catch up. I never want to make him wait for me again, if I can help it.

❆

On Tuesday, we're wrapping up for the night when pounding at the back door rings out again. Austin gets there first and greets the visitor. "Susie," he says, without any surprise in his tone. Apparently, this is how she makes an entrance.

"Oh good, I caught you all before you left." Her eyes bounce from me to Austin and back again. "They were able to clear the steps of the ice with some ice melt and help from the sun showing its face again today. You can go up and grab whatever you need now."

I breathe a sigh of relief. I'm getting by with the few things we grabbed the other night, but I'm anxious to check on my Santa suits. Plus, days without yoga and constantly in Austin's presence have really given me the need to unwind.

"Oh no, I'm sorry, Brody. You can go grab your things, but you're not going to be able to stay." Susie misreads my reaction as expecting to get my space back. I try not to let more relief show at the prospect of more time with Austin. "Between the carpet and drywall damage and the time of year, I think it's best if you plan not to be able to stay there again until your time with us as Santa is through."

She looks at Austin expectantly, and I fight the urge to join her. I don't want to put pressure on him he doesn't need. "Let me know if I need to put out the call for another room or place to stay. I'm sure there are plenty of people willing to put up the Santa who's done such wonderful things for all the children who have come to see him." I bite back a laugh—subtlety is not Susie's strong suit.

"No, it's fine," Austin says, quicker than I expected. "I've got the space, and Brody's already set up there. It may not be the most comfortable bed in the world, but I think it's okay."

"Well, dear, you could always spring for a new mattress. How old is the one you're sleeping on now?" Susie's eyes glint with a devilish twinkle.

"What? No. We don't share a mattress. It's a pullout. In the guest room. I guess we could get a topper . . ." Austin trails off as he realizes he's been got. I'm not successful at stifling a laugh this time, which turns his glare on me.

"In any case, I'm glad to hear Santa's being well taken care of. You boys let me know if you need any help loading up Brody's stuff. I'll come to the bottom of the stairs and cheer you on." And with far less fanfare than she entered with, Susie disappears back into the night.

"I guess we better go get changed and then go get your stuff," Austin says.

"I guess so," I say. Austin walks ahead of me toward the back door, and Jimmy sticks his hand out low for a high five as I walk past. I barely even feel bad about returning it.

Luckily, the pipe burst away from where most of my stuff is stored, so beyond everything having a bit of a damp feel, nothing is ruined. Some clothes may need a few spins through a hot water cycle to remove a faint smell of mildew, but with our day off tomorrow, I should have the time. I didn't want to open the bags holding my suits in that environment, and my knee bounces nervously on the drive back from Holly Ridge, everything I brought with me piled in the back of Austin's Bronco.

"Where did you find your suits? How did you learn how to take care of them?" Austin asks. I smile. First, because he's doing a great job of skirting around asking me flat out how I ended up a professional Santa. And second, because I didn't mention my anxiety around the state of the Santa suits, but he still figured it out.

"There are professional Santa schools in various places around the country—a big one in New York. They have a lot of resources for where to get quality materials, plus it's a friendly community. For the most part, fellow Santas are more than willing to help."

"Imagine that—people who play Santa being a welcoming and friendly bunch," Austin says, his tone a little sarcastic.

"There are definitely folks who take it really seriously and are territorial of the yearly gigs and connections they've made. But most of us are there because we want to feel good about what we do, professionally or as a side gig, and want to spread the joy."

"You're right. I'm sorry for making a joke. You definitely don't want Santa to be a cranky guy or a drunk."

"Another perk of being involved in more professional Santa organizations, like the schools. Those who are in the know look for vetted professionals to avoid those types of awkward scenarios. Bad cookies can still slip through, or people go through hard times, of course, but it helps."

We're silent as we cross into Winterberry Glen. Once again, I take in the great job they've done of decorating the streets.

"They've asked me to consider doing some lectures next summer," I say quietly. It's the first time I've told anyone. "They want me to talk a little bit about how I started the charitable arm of my business, so others can consider it, even on a much smaller scale."

"Brody, that's awesome. I really think you're doing something great with your charity—kids are getting the joy from meeting you and also getting access to other resources at the same time, without even knowing it."

I nod. "I had the means to make it happen. I wanted to do some good for once, after feeling so bad for so long." We're parked now, and Austin waits quietly to see if I'll continue. After a few moments, he breaks the silence, clearing his throat.

"Well, let's go get your suits looked at and start a load of your clothes. You can do a search to see which dry cleaners have the processes you'll need, and then I can vet if they're trustworthy or not."

We go up and get started. The suits are in great shape, thanks to the heavy-duty bags I keep them in. I still want to get them cleaned, along with the one I've been wearing for the past few days, to be sure no musty smells creep in. Austin approves one of the places I find, right down the street, and promises we can go first thing in the morning and get a same-day job from them. Turns out, while he never worked there, he did work for the auto shop the family owns a few years back, so they'll give him as many favors as he wants.

Leftovers from last night's chicken have been cleared and we're sitting on the couch, each with a beer in hand. Austin gave me the remote and didn't complain when I put on a Hallmark Christmas movie. I'd go as far as to say he's even enjoying the hijinks of three brothers trying to care for a baby dropped off on their front porch.

"Why don't you have a Christmas tree?" I ask during the next commercial break. "Or any decorations, really?"

He shrugs, taking a sip of his beer, his lips curling tantalizing around the long neck bottle. "I typically spend Christmas at my mom's and we decorate there. I'm usually at the Christmas tree farm for such long hours too—I get my fill of pine."

"But you're not there this year?" I ask. Austin asked a follow-up question last night, so I'm choosing to believe those are in play for this unofficial game of Twenty Questions we're volleying back and forth.

Austin picks at the label on his bottle. "No. They needed to downsize after the fall festival. I had seniority with how many years I've worked for them, but a young kid needed a job more. I asked them to give it to him instead." He shrugs, like willingly putting himself out of a job in the middle of winter is no big deal. I wouldn't have expected him to do anything else.

"We should go get you a tree tomorrow. Is the lot open? I'll pitch in."

He rolls his eyes. "I didn't say I can't afford a tree."

I put a hand on his arm, hoping I didn't offend him. "No, I know. But I meant I'm staying in your space, rent free, and I'm the one suggesting you decorate. I can pitch in."

"You were staying at Jitters rent free too, right? Would you have helped Susie get a tree?"

"If I believed an iota of undecorated space existed in Jitters to put a tree, absolutely I would." We both laugh—I can't say for sure, but I imagine Susie starts decorating on November first.

"And you want to decorate a tree, do more Christmassy stuff on your day off?" His eyes meet mine then, and I read the doubt in his eyes he's not saying. Is it smart, is it safe, for us to do such a domestic thing together?

I keep my tone light. "C'mon, I'm a professional Santa. Of course I want to help decorate." Our eyes stay locked, and I hope he reads in them what I'm not saying. For you, Austin? I'll do anything.

Epistolary Interlude #1

COLE

When were you planning on telling me Brody is staying at your place?

AUSTIN

Um, right now? I guess. I honestly thought you already knew.

COLE

How would I already know if my best friend doesn't tell me anything?

AUSTIN

. . .

BLAIRE

Okay, but listen, you had such a rough week with the twins being sick while I was gone, and we had such a nice weekend. And honestly, can you blame me for not telling you?

COLE

If I had slept more than three hours in a row
for the past four months, I'd have more energy
to be mad about this.

BLAIRE

I know, Pookie.

AUSTIN

I love it when Mom and Dad don't fight.

COLE

You did not carry my children, mister. I can
find the energy to be mad at you.

AUSTIN

Listen, it's fine! I'm fine. It'll all be fine.

BLAIRE

If you say it enough, it'll come true?

AUSTIN

Something like that.

COLE

Well, you should get out of the house
tomorrow on your day off, get some space.
Want to come over?

AUSTIN

Can I take a snow check?

COLE

What are you guys doing?

AUSTIN

We're going to go get a Christmas tree and
some decorations. He thought it would be fun
to make my place more festive.

> Just a casual day between two roommates who used to see each other naked on the regular. It'll be fine.

BLAIRE

> Awe, how cute! Send pics?

COLE

> I don't know what I'm going to do with either one of you.

From: admin@walkersantaco.com
To: brody@walkersantaco.com
Re: Updates

Dear Mr. Walker,

Please see attached the reports of donations received in November. We're up 27% from this point last year.

Also attached is an updated schedule of assignments for the rest of December for you to approve.

Finally, I'm forwarding the feedback we got from the job Ted Baker did last week. He has several high-profile appearances coming up—would you like to make any changes?

Please let me know if there's anything else you need.

Best,
Monica

Chapter 13

Austin

After cooking a big breakfast, Brody is bouncing with energy for us to head out and go shopping for a tree. His excitement is infectious—the part I didn't say last night is it seemed too depressing to me to decorate my place when I didn't have anyone else to share it with. I have a roommate now—*roommate, sure, Austin*, I scoff internally—what harm could a little extra Christmas cheer do?

After dropping off the dry cleaning, we drive forty-five minutes to where there are a few places close together, so we can have more options than what Wally World would have. Brody suggests a pause in the official count of our questions game, so we can discover our decoration compatibility.

"White lights or multicolored lights?" he asks.

"White lights, definitely." I turn down the Christmas channel he put on so I can hear better.

"Oh, wrong. But it's okay, you'll learn." I laugh. Brody hasn't allowed himself to be this free around me yet. It's hard to ignore how charming it is.

"Candy canes or popcorn string?" He moves on to the next question.

"Candy canes, for sure. Way less work."

He nods. "Smart. We're getting a late start, a good time to be efficient. How do you feel about inflatables?"

I shoot a quick glance at him, glad we're at a red light before pulling into the first store. "I live in an apartment . . ."

"You have a balcony!" he says, like it's completely reasonable to go from suggesting we get a tree to decorate to purchasing an inflatable to put on a balcony barely big enough for two people to sit on at the same time.

"What happened to only getting a tree?"

His eyes twinkle as I turn the car off. "I never said just a tree. We'll walk through the inflatables section, see if anything catches your eye."

"Okay." I get out of the car and look back at him across the hood as he does the same. "But I don't think I'm going to find anything I like."

"Never say never," he says, full of confidence, taking off at a brisk walk for the entrance not related to the temperature outside.

I chuckle and follow, realizing I'm simply along for the ride.

Hours later, we have a six-foot Douglas fir strapped to the roof of my vehicle and bags of lights, ornaments, extension cords, and, yes, a box holding an inflatable fill the back seat and cargo area. I turn off the ignition and sit back in exhaustion. "How am I more tired now than I am at the end of a day playing an elf?"

"Perk up," he says, patting my leg. It's not the first time we've touched each other casually today, but like every time before, I feel his touch long after he's removed his hand. "We'll unload, I'll put dinner in the oven, and then we can relax with a nice glass of the eggnog you grabbed until we eat. You'll feel better with your blood sugar up and be ready to decorate."

"Or the whisky and eggnog combo will serve its purpose," I mutter.

"Whatever works!" Brody closes the passenger door behind him and goes to wait by the liftgate. For the umpteenth time, I smile at how happy he's been all day—at how much fun we've both had spending time together. He's right, it's going to be a lot of fun to see the fruits of our labor after dinner.

Food in the oven and eggnog poured over ice, we head into the living room, but neither of us sits down to rest. He starts pulling things out of shopping bags. I snag the inflatable and an extension cord and head toward the balcony.

"Inflatable first thing, huh?" he teases.

I shrug, trying to keep my expression indifferent. "It'll be fully dark soon. Figured it would be good to get out here while I can still sort of see what I'm doing."

"Okaaay," he says in a tone telling me I'm full of shit, but I decide I don't care. Putting an inflatable of the Abominable Snow Monster from claymation Rudolph onto my balcony is going to be awesome. I won't deny it.

A few minutes later, the Bumble is tied down, fully inflated, and lit up. I put it on a timer, so it'll turn on while we're still at work, but I wonder if it's too much to run down and see how it looks.

I close the door and find Brody climbing down from a chair. "Whatcha doing?" I ask.

"Hanging this mistletoe they threw in for free when we checked out. The rest of the ceilings are too high to reach, so I thought right over the hallway would work."

"Oh, good to know," I laugh awkwardly. "Be sure to steer clear of that—one person in the hallway at a time."

Brody's face falls, and I curse myself. He never said anything about enforcing it. Even if he did mean it to be a kissing spot, I didn't need to be quite so careless in my response.

"Right. Sure." He tries to recover. "I thought it was kind of funny, and they gave it to us for free, so . . . But I'll take it down." He moves to climb onto the chair again.

"No, it's fine. It looks good there. I'm . . . I'm going to run down to see how the inflatable looks from the street." Without another word, I flee out the door and down the stairs, not even stopping for my coat.

As I stand on the sidewalk, shivering and staring at a three-foot-tall Abominable growling at me, I feel like I deserve this. Things are going so well between us. I don't think it's a good idea to get romantically involved with Brody again—he has his business and his life he'll be going back to in three weeks—doesn't mean I have to be an ass about it. I look up at the sky, hoping there will be an answer written among the stars. Instead, grey cloud cover mocks me and tells me I need to go clean my mess.

I climb back up the stairs slowly and cautiously open the door. In the past when we fought, Before Brody would go to the gym or throw himself into work to blow off steam. This Brody doesn't have a job he can disappear to. Maybe he'll be hiding in his room doing some yoga, and I'll be left to stare at the tied up tree, reminding myself what an idiot I am.

Brody pops his head out of the kitchen, a freshly poured eggnog in his hand. "Dinner will be ready in two minutes." His eyes give nothing away, but I wince at the big gulp he takes of his drink. It's been a while since we had lunch—I'm glad dinner will be ready soon.

I sit on the couch to give him space, listening as he bustles around and pulls the baking sheet out of the oven. Right when I'm about to take a peek and see if it's safe for me to come make a plate of my own, Brody appears next to me with two plates in hand.

"Oh, you didn't need to bring me a plate. I could have served myself," I say, taking the extended plate and silverware.

He shrugs. "I was bringing my own over, so figured I'd grab yours too. Oh! My drink!" He goes back for the glass, and I notice it's full to the brim again. Fuck, I need to grow some balls and apologize.

I turn the TV to whatever Hallmark Christmas movie is on now, but otherwise we eat in silence. Brody doesn't even seem to be paying attention to the movie. It's beyond time for me to speak up.

"Hey, I'm . . . I'm sorry about what I said about the mistletoe earlier. It was uncalled for."

He shrugs and avoids my eyes. "You were speaking your truth. I should have asked before I hung it. It's your apartment."

Twisting my body, I turn more to face him. "It's not that—I panicked in the moment. Today was great, and we've had some good days and good talks together. But I don't think it's a good idea for us to get romantically involved again. So, when you brought up mistletoe, my mind went straight to kissing you. I didn't think before I spoke. I'm sorry."

He nods, taking the last bite of his food before putting the plate on the coffee table, picking up his drink before he leans back.

"So, you think every kiss has to be romantic?"

I startle, surprised by his question. "No, I don't. But don't you?"

Brody shakes his head. "Not anymore." His tone is weathered and weary.

I sit with what he said for a moment. The Brody I knew only got physically involved in relationships. He said he couldn't separate sex from emotion. Maybe I didn't fully consider what it did to him to leave what we had behind.

"Oh." I'm not quite sure what else to say. The ice in Brody's glass clinks, and I decide I might need another eggnog to get through the evening too. I stand up, grabbing our plates. "Can I get you a refill?"

"No." He shakes his head. "I'm already feeling a little reckless. Better call it quits—and it's against my code as Santa to be hungover."

Existing hungover is miserable, I can't imagine trying to be Santa. "That's smart." I put our dishes in the sink and pour myself a drink, taking it easy on the whisky.

I sit back down, not watching the movie on the TV. I'm about to suggest we at least get the tree in the stand, so it can have water and rest its branches overnight when Brody breaks the silence.

"When's the last time you had sex?"

I have no idea how to answer. "Is this an official question on the record?"

"Sure, why not." He shrugs and takes the last sip of his drink.

No good can come of this conversation, but apparently the whisky has me feeling a little reckless too. "About two weeks. The night before Thanksgiving."

He nods. "It was Halloween weekend for me. I was dressed as Captain Kirk and went home with a Luke Skywalker." He snorts, and the image would be funny in any other situation, but the vision of Brody, naked with someone else, isn't funny at all.

"Oh." I grasp for something to say. "You don't dress up as Santa for Halloween?" *Anything* else might have been better.

"Those suits are way too expensive to go out in. And no. I guess I've always thought of Santa as a sexless being. But it probably would pull pretty well, the ultimate Daddy fantasy."

I choke on the last sip of my eggnog. Daddies have never been my thing, but combining Brody as a bear, plus the way he smells all woodsy, how his beard would tickle along my skin, and the confidence of a daddy is doing something for me. Something very specific, like hardening my dick.

"We could, you know," Brody says, and I've completely lost track of the conversation now.

"We could what?"

"Have sex. The beard comes for free this time of year."

I blink at him a few times. "No, I don't think that's a good idea."

"Because you don't think we should get involved romantically?"

"For one reason, sure."

"I know you have sex just to have sex, Austin. I do too. With having to chauffeur me around, the packed schedule of the workshop, and the idea of your ex in the next room throwing ice on everything, it's going to be hard to pick up for a few weeks."

He's not wrong, but shockingly, I hadn't given it a thought until he brought it up. As someone who has a decent amount of sex, you'd think it would have crossed my mind before now. But it never did.

"Santa season is definitely my driest time of the year." My hands curl in on themselves, hearing Brody being so casual about sex with someone else. Me having sex with other people doesn't seem to bother him, but apparently I'm not as evolved. "It could be a convenient solution."

The air between us ripples with tension. I see his chest start to move up and down faster and use every inch of willpower at my disposal not to look down and see if his dick is in the same state as mine.

A car horn blares on the TV and breaks the spell. "I think this might be the eggnog talking," I say, trying to keep my tone gentle. "I would be taking advantage of you if I agreed to this right now, tonight. I'm going to put the tree in the stand. We can let the branches rest overnight and finish decorating after work tomorrow. You go ahead and go to bed. I promise you won't want this in the morning."

Brody stands, not saying anything else. I hope I didn't ruin what we've built by turning him down, but what I said is true. He's had too much whisky to do anything consensual tonight.

He stops in the entrance to the hallway, right under the mistletoe that started all this trouble. "You're a good guy, Austin. You know that?"

I shrug, not sure how to answer.

"And what if I still want it in the morning?" he asks, his back to me.

"You won't," I say, convinced what I'm saying is true.

He walks away, and I just barely hear him saying, "I wouldn't count on it," before he shuts his door.

I rush through getting the tree into the stand and getting the ropes cut off, before adding water to the base. Convinced it's not going to fall over in the night, I hurry through my bedtime routine and shut myself in my room, cut off from any temptations or bad decisions.

On the dresser, I grab my bottle of melatonin for the first time since Brody came to stay with me. I haven't had as much trouble sleeping since he arrived, but I don't trust my mind not to whir with thoughts I don't want to be having when I lay down tonight. Between the whisky and the gummies, I should be lights out in no time. I drop my clothes on the floor next to the bed and crawl into the sheets in only my Christmas tree boxer briefs. My eyes close and, as I hoped, I have no trouble drifting off.

What I can't control is the thoughts my brain conjures up while I'm asleep. They're filled with images of Brody, dancing in a crowded club as Captain Kirk, beckoning me to come dance with him. The same expression he wore when I shut down his mistletoe appears when I say no.

Somehow, that image morphs into him straddling me, wearing only a Santa hat. It feels so good to touch his skin. My hands rub up his thighs, the hair there tickling my skin, over the swell of his stomach. I stop at his nipples, giving each one a tweak before tangling my fingers in the hair at the back of his head and pulling his mouth to mine. As he slowly descends, his hips grind down once, our dicks rubbing together in a way that has me groaning his name right before his lips consume mine.

My eyes shoot open, and I sit up, breathing hard. It felt like calling out his name is what woke me up, but in the space between dreaming and waking, I'm not positive I did or not. The floor creaks right outside my door, and I hold my breath, but Brody's footsteps move away from our rooms and out to the kitchen. The noises of him making coffee travel back down the hall, and I look at the time on my phone. The 10:00 has me jumping out of bed, having to tuck my morning wood back under the elastic of my briefs from where the head is peeking out. I'm sure Brody's been up for a while, and I missed him showering. Normally, I'd check, but this situation with my dick isn't going away without some attention. With the short time we have before we need to be in Holly Ridge, it will have to be a quick jerk in the shower. Time to multitask.

Opening the door a crack, I stick my head out and smell the fresh coffee dripping into the carafe, accompanied by the sounds of Brody doing the dishes. I don't even take the time to feel bad that he's cleaning up after he cooked last night. I rush to the bathroom and rest against the door when it's shut safely behind me. One deep breath, then two, before I move to turn on the shower faucet. While I wait for it to get warm, I take myself in my hand and give a quick, firm stroke. Sparks shoot down my dick toward my balls. No, this won't take long at all. Which is what I need since I have no time.

Shower curtain closed, and my hand bracing on the back wall as hot water sluices down my back, I curl the palm of my hand around my cock once more. My arm moves with a tentative stroke. I pause to gather a pump of body wash and turn my attention to the matter at hand when I hear it. A quick knock on the door, followed by the creak of the hinges and the sound of Brody saying my name.

"Austin?"

Chapter 14

I can't believe how late I slept. When I read 9:40 on my phone, I think it must be p.m. and all the memories of propositioning Austin last night were from a post-dinner nap. God, I can't believe I did that. I run through the memories of our conversation, his objection to kissing me, and the strong pour of whisky I mixed to dull the hurt. And then my suggesting we could have casual sex.

It is true I've only had casual sex since I started law school. The idea of letting someone in again, letting them have a chance of derailing the plan, hurt too much. And in those moments, it felt nice to be held, even if it never felt as right as when Austin held me.

My dick hardens more thinking about touching Austin again. I throw the covers off and pull on a pair of sweatpants to go get some coffee. I'm sure Austin's been up for hours, but hopefully some is still hot.

My eyes land on the closed door of Austin's room. How is he going to act toward me today? Will he want to pretend it never happened? Want to talk *again* about how it isn't a good idea?

A sound comes from behind the door, a moan I thought I'd

only hear again in my dreams. My feet take me closer to the door of their own accord, straining, wondering if I'll hear it again. And then.

"Brody!" followed by the squeak of a bed when someone sits up quickly.

He said my name. A dream about me is what caused that moan.

I try to back away softly and slowly, wincing when I hit the floorboard that seems to creak every time. I give up the quiet act and hurry into the kitchen, hoping he will think I stepped on it in the normal course of leaving my room. Not listening at the door.

My movements toward the coffee maker are trancelike. Does it mean anything if he's having a sexual dream about me hours after I bring up the idea of us adding benefits to our rediscovered friendship? Can I even refer to what we've rebuilt as a friendship?

Water overflows out of the carafe and over my hand, setting me in motion again. While I pour the water into the coffeemaker and grounds into the filter, I try to set myself straight. I shouldn't read too much into what I overheard. Austin can't be held responsible for what his dream self conjures up. We did have some pretty fantastic sex back in the day. And I put the thought of us having sex again into his head. Doesn't mean he *wanted* it there.

I move over to doing the dishes once the coffee starts brewing. Keeping my hands busy and my mind empty will help me from getting any big ideas about what his moan could have meant. I'll finish up here, make myself a big cup of the coffee smelling like it has the potential to erase last night's bad decisions, and follow Austin's lead.

The sound of hurried footsteps in the hall is followed by the bathroom door closing. A second later, the water turns on and I hang my head over the sink. No amount of dish doing can stop the images of Austin, standing underneath the shower, water flowing over his broad shoulders, down over that bubble butt I want to take a bite out of. His back to the spray, drops of water sneaking over his chest, trickling down his abs to the patch of hair he always kept trim, around his thick, long cock. Would he stroke it once, twice, out of habit? Or did the dream he had—whether he wanted it or not—leave him needing relief?

My feet start moving toward the bathroom, all thoughts of following Austin's lead forgotten. He hadn't believed I would still want him, want this, in the morning. What better time to make sure he knows than right now?

I take a deep breath, knock quickly on the door and open it without waiting for a reply. If he tells me to go, I won't hesitate to turn around. But I have to try.

"Austin?" I say, hoping sounds of the shower drown out the hint of a quiver my voice holds.

Nothing comes from the other side of the curtain other than the splash of water and the scent of his spicy body wash. I curse internally, reaching for the doorknob behind me when—

"Brody." It's not a question or a curse. My name coming from his lips sounds almost like a prayer. An admission he shouldn't want this, but he does. I tug down my briefs and sweatpants, letting them pool next to Austin's briefs on the floor. My shirt comes next, and I cross the small bathroom in two steps. Curling my fingers around the edge of the curtain, I pause for a moment, making sure he can see my intent, giving him another chance to stop this.

He says nothing, so slower than I've ever pulled back a curtain in my life, I reveal an image destined for spank bank eternity: a dripping wet Austin, exactly how I imagined him. He's bracing himself on the back wall of the shower, a hand curled loosely around that gorgeous cock. It's longer and thicker than I remember, and my memories are plenty generous. His abs are clenched tight with the restraint of not stroking, not chasing the pleasure I interrupted.

"Fuck, you're gorgeous." I breathe, unable to tear my eyes away from the sight, filling my lungs with the deepest breath I've taken in ten fucking years.

His eyes trace me while I map his body, and they meet mine

then. "You're not doing so bad yourself over there." His eyes flick back to where my own cock continues to fill, shorter but thicker along my thigh. In the next moment, he traces his gaze upward, over where my stomach rounds and hair grows thick on my chest. I blink in succession several times—so focused on setting my eyes on this beautiful man, I forgot how much I've changed since he last saw me like this.

Something must pass over my face giving away my thoughts, and he shakes his head fiercely, standing up straight. "No, don't. This is you—I see you."

I'm getting close to my emotional limit, which should be very low, considering this is just sex. Time to get us back on track. "Can I?" I gesture to the spot between his body and the wall, making my intentions clear.

"Brody—" His voice sounds pained, and I think he's about to pull back, return to the safety of the lines he's drawn since I got back to town. "I don't think we have time."

My smile is wicked as I step over the edge of the tub, my body as close to his without allowing us to touch. "Let me worry about that."

I sink to my knees, watching Austin shuttle his fist up and down his cock, unable to hold back. Encircling his wrist gently, I pull it away. I'd love to spend ages down here, taking him in, reveling in how good he'll feel in my mouth, but he's not wrong. Time is short, and hopefully there will be a next time.

I lean forward, and circle the head of his cock with my tongue, watching as his eyes flutter closed and his body shivers in response to the stimulation. One hand grips his thigh for leverage, and the other holds at the base of his cock, moving with my mouth as I take him deeper with each stroke. Opening my throat, the tip of his dick slides deepest yet, and my hand moves from the base of his cock to tug on his balls while I swallow. His eyes shoot open at the same time as he slaps a hand back on the wall of the shower. Eyes locked on mine, I see him starting to fray at the edges.

I'd love to bring him right to the brink then push him back to the ledge, but a voice in the back of my mind tells me, "Santa had his elf's cock down his throat," isn't a great reason for holding up the crowds. My hand moves down to wrap around my own cock, stiff and leaking. I set a rhythm with my mouth and mimic with my own strokes. Austin's other hand comes up and wraps in my hair. My grip on his thigh tightens, letting him know he can let go. Austin's hips thrust into my mouth while I hold myself open, once, twice, and then he's pouring down the back of my throat.

The taste of him is enough to send me over the edge. I groan with my own orgasm as I come onto the tub floor. Austin's eyes widen as the vibrations extend his release, and I feel some of his cum start to trickle out of my mouth. My mouth slackens, letting it drip toward my chin as Austin pulls out. He swipes the trail upward with his finger, pushing on my lip until I open for him slightly. He catches every last drop from my face, making sure none of it goes to waste, and my dick starts to perk up again at the move.

Austin's chest heaves up and down, his eyes still on mine. I push off the floor, bringing myself closer to his full height. For a moment, we say nothing. "I told you I'd still want it."

Austin laughs and steps back under the shower stream, his eyes blinking as if to clear his mind. "A very effective demonstration to prove your point. And with your effectiveness, we may not be late after all." He hands me the body wash, then grabs the shampoo for himself. A quick lather in his hair before he tips his head back again to wash it clean. All the while, I'm standing there in awe, and a little cold, the body wash bottle tight in my grip.

Hair rinsed, he steps out of the shower and grabs his towel off the rack, drying off before wrapping it around his waist. I've led us here—I need him to show me where we go next.

He jerks his head toward the stream of water he abandoned. "Get moving. We'll talk after we've spent the day around small children. I promise." With one more appreciative look at my ass, he turns and leaves the bathroom.

I jolt into action, washing my body and hair on autopilot. He's not wrong. We barely have time for a normal shower each, let alone any bathroom recreation. Still, something twists in the bottom of my stomach. Seizing the moment seemed so right when the shower started, but now with the water starting to run cold, it's taking my emotions with it. Was it a mistake to do this when we didn't have time to lay down any ground rules after? Was it a good idea at all?

Leaving the shower, I hustle to my room to get dressed, trying to steer my thoughts in a more productive direction that won't leave me a mopey Santa all day. It's 11:15 am when I finally head to the door to grab my coat. Austin comes up behind me with two travel mugs of coffee. "I'll call Jitters on the way over and ask them to have something for us to run in and grab. Can't be Santa on an empty stomach." His wink tells me he remembers what my stomach is full of, and my spirits lift. Maybe we can do this. Maybe there doesn't need to be some big conversation.

Later, when I've checked in with Jimmy and am getting myself into Santa's chair at 11:59, I almost can't believe we've made it.

"I'll take that." Austin walks up next to me and holds out his hand for the Jitter's bag I forgot I'm still holding.

"Oh, thanks," I say, surprised he's the one asking for my garbage. "No door duty today?"

"Nah," he says. "I'd rather be over here."

We're still staring at each other, smiles bordering on dopey, when Minh rings the bell by the front door to signal the start of the day, and voices fill the workshop. The sugarplums dancing in my stomach are there from the prospect of some good sex, I tell myself. No other reason.

A few minutes later, Austin hits me with his megawatt smile as he helps the first child off my lap and over to Jimmy's station. Sex sugarplums or not, I may be in big trouble.

Chapter 15

Austin

As the day wears on, I notice Brody starting to lose some of his sparkle. I don't know anyone else can see it—the kids are still climbing off his lap smiling and laughing, thrilled with how Santa responded to what they want for Christmas. But even if he hadn't had my dick in his mouth eight hours ago, I would know something is off.

I shoot him a subtle thumbs up behind my body when we have an hour left before closing time, and he gives a smile and a small nod, before wincing at the head movement. Migraine. I recognize the signs from when Mom would get them during her treatment. I wonder what his triggers are. Stress? Not enough to eat? Change in the weather? My stomach twists with the thought stress or food might be the cause now, as they could both be considered my fault. I keep a close watch on him for the rest of the shift. Are his eyes taking longer to open with each blink? I really might be losing it now.

The door closes behind the final family, and Brody tilts his head back against the chair and pulls his hat down over his eyes. I exchange a worried look with Jimmy and head over, putting my hand gently on his arm to try to not startle him.

"Hey, Austin," he says, before I even say anything, his voice weary.

"How'd you know it was me?" I say, migraine temporarily forgotten.

"I've smelled like you all day." His small smile calls me back to how he got that way. "The smell got stronger when you came over." I match his smile, though it quickly turns into a frown when he grimaces again.

"Migraine, right? Let's get moving so we can get you home."

He sits up straight, trying to put on a game face. "No, we need to pitch in to cleanup. Friday tomorrow, means even more people than today."

"I'm pretty sure everyone wants Santa to be in tip-top shape for a busy Friday." My eyes bounce around the room, and as expected, most everyone is listening in, before taking in his grey expression again. "I'm pretty sure they'd want you to go home and get some rest." I'm ready to plead with my eyes for support, but everyone's nodding when I look back up.

Brody realizes all eyes are on us too. "Okay, but coffees are on me tomorrow."

I smile as everyone does a silent cheer, not wanting to add noise and make things any worse.

"Let's go, big guy." I pull Brody to his feet and help him into his coat before grabbing mine. Our pace back to the gym is steady, until he stops still at the door.

"Everything okay?" I ask, looking back at his face scrunched up in pain.

"Building myself up to step into a fluorescent light hellscape."

I pull my keys out of my pocket. "Go ahead and get in the car, suit and all. I'll go grab our stuff and be out in a second." He starts to protest. "We got those suits cleaned yesterday for a reason, right? Go."

He takes the keys and smiles weakly before heading to the car. I hustle to grab our stuff, leaving the tights on but throwing on a sweatshirt, so I can make it even speedier.

Brody's eyes are closed and his head is back against the seat when I climb into the Bronco. "Making it so if we get pulled over, we look like we just ran away from the North Pole?" he asks without opening his eyes.

"One should never cosplay and ride in a car alone." I'm not sure how he knew I didn't change fully, but not surprised either. He seems to be in tune with me in a way no one, except maybe Cole, ever has been.

"Let's get you home," I say, easing my SUV from the parking lot and praying for green lights and no bumps on the way.

"Go lay down, I'll be right there," I say once we get back to the apartment. My eyes catch on the empty Christmas tree I definitely need to straighten before I go to bed tonight. We still have plenty of time to decorate and enjoy it before Christmas. Trimming can wait for another night. I hang both our coats up and head to the kitchen to grab an electrolyte packet, chocolate, and run a washcloth under some warm water.

Brody's laying on his bed, Santa pants around his ankles with his feet on the floor. His coat is open, but still on his shoulders, and his arm thrown over his head.

"It's a real doozy, isn't it?" I lean down to undo his boots and slide them off as gently as I can.

"Yeah, I haven't had one this bad in a couple of months. They're mostly controlled with medicine, but sometimes a perfect storm brings one on." His voice is mumbled behind his sleeve.

"Is it okay if I take your pants the rest of the way off?" I ask, unable to keep the humor out of my voice.

"Not how I pictured you asking that question," he groans, lifting his feet slightly to help me free them from the pants before we swing his legs back up onto the mattress.

"I brought you a few things. Do you have medicine to take once they start?"

He eases his way into sitting, his eyes still closed against the ceiling light he must have turned on out of habit. I reach over to the wall and flick it off, letting the light from the hallway and the inflatable through the window closest to the balcony filter through.

"Yeah, it's in my toiletry bag on the dresser." With his jacket finally removed, he hunches over with his head in his hands, fingers massaging his temples.

I take his words as an invitation to go through his things and unzip the bag to find four orange bottles. The first I pick up is his PrEP prescription, information I tuck away for later. The second bottle has a prescription name I don't recognize. The third label reads Xanax, so I grab the fourth bottle once I see it's another name I don't know, figuring one of these two has to be the winner.

"Here—I'm not sure which one you need." Brody picks his head up, his eyes open only the slightest amount until it sinks in the room is dark. He grabs both bottles, uncapping one.

"This'll do it, though it's going to knock me out, too." He puts the pill in his mouth, then looks around in panic.

"Oh, I got you." I pick the electrolyte drink up off the floor where I put it when I came in, twisting the cap off and handing it to him. He takes a deliberate swallow and then drains most of the rest of the bottle without taking another breath.

"Thanks, that should help it along." He starts to burrow himself in bed, and I stand awkwardly, not sure what to do with myself.

"I, uh, grabbed you some chocolate too. It helped my mom when she got migraines during treatment—some mixture of caffeine and a natural chocolate high, I think." I hold out the miniature bars in Christmas-themed paper, and he cups them in his hand.

"I'll never turn down chocolate," he says, propping his head up slightly on his pillows. "Thanks for getting me back here in one piece—it can be a nightmare to navigate the simplest things on your own when the pain's really taken hold."

"Of course, I wish I could do more," I say, settling myself next to his feet on the bed.

"I have about five more minutes before these meds knock me out for the next ten to twelve hours. So, if there's anything you want to say to me, I may or may not remember it in the morning, now's the time."

The light from the hallway reflects in his eyes, their seriousness a mismatch from the lightness of his tone.

"Ilikedwhathappenedthismorning," I say, all in a rush. A lot of effort had gone into not dwelling on Brody draining my cock in the shower this morning while we were around kids and families all day. "I might like it to happen again."

A pleased smile breaks onto Brody's face. "I know I'd like for it to happen again. You know, orgasms are a scientifically proven method of relieving headache pain."

I squeeze his foot before standing to hover over him. "I think a less than five-minute window before you're unconscious puts you out of commission. Sleep, Brody. We've got time."

I lean down and brush a kiss along his forehead, watching as his eyes flutter closed and stay closed.

"Night," I say softly, standing up straight and watching him lie there peacefully.

"Night," he murmurs, before his breathing evens out and the medicine takes him under.

After gathering the pieces of his suit from the floor and hanging them in the closet, I walk out of the room and shut the door softly behind me. I think about what I said to Brody.

We've got time. Am I lying to myself, and even worse, to him?

The next morning I'm up at a much more normal time, in part because I didn't sleep well. My mind raced with thoughts of the man across the hall. How it felt when he touched me. How badly I want him to do it again and touch him in return. But by not putting a stop to this, am I setting us up for a world of hurt when he eventually goes back to New York? Well, Stamford. But the point being, not here.

When I decide I can't stare at the ceiling any longer, I get up and head to the kitchen, managing to avoid the creaky floorboard. It's only been about nine hours since Brody fell asleep, and I don't want to interrupt his recovery. I stare into the fridge, trying to decide what sounds appetizing for breakfast. The urge I have isn't to eat, but to untangle this Brody mess in my head.

Right on cue, my phone pings with a text from Cole checking to see if we're still on for dinner on Sunday. What's the point of having a best friend who never sleeps if you can't show up at their front door with all your problems?

"Austin?" Cole answers my call after the first ring, his voice concerned.

"If I bring coffee and pastries, can I crash your morning routine?"

"Even without coffee and pastries. You bring that cute ass over here with the gossip you've been denying me, and you've got a deal," he responds, and I hear Blaire laugh in the background.

"You've been living in Holly Ridge for too long, my man," I say. "See you within the hour?"

"See you then."

I jump into action, putting the coffeepot on a timer to brew so it will be ready for when Brody wakes up. Not wanting to risk the noise of the shower, I throw some clothes into a bag, figuring I can shower at Blaire and Cole's or worst case, at the high school, before I change.

Back in the living room, I stop short, realizing I've been on my own for too long. How will Brody get to Holly Ridge if I take the car? After a moment's consideration, I turn over a notice from the building about snow maintenance and write a note.

> Brody,
> I hope your head's better. I didn't want
> to risk waking you up, so I went to Cole's for
> a late breakfast. Here are the keys. I'll see
> you in the locker room at 11:30.
> X, Austin
> P.S. Don't freak out I'm not here. We'll
> talk soon.

Setting the keys next to the note, I pull out my phone to order a rideshare. While I wait on the curb for the driver to pick me up, I worry over what I wrote. I didn't want to promise him everything is okay, because I'm not sure it is. But talking to Cole will be one of the best ways to get me there.

I knock on the door, and moments later, Blaire and Melody open the door to greet me.

"Uncle Austin's here," she says, bouncing the happy little girl.

"With bribes," I say, in the same overly excited tone.

"Uncle Austin's the best." She shuts the door behind me and embraces me in a side hug with her empty arm. "I'm heading out in a minute, but could wait a little while for a hug and a peppermint mocha." I point to one of the cups with the hand holding the bag of pastries, and Blaire works it out of the cup holder.

"I think it's more the coffee than the hug," I tease, and she smiles slyly.

"I mean, isn't peppermint mocha a hug in a cup?" She turns her attention to her daughter. "Let's get you back to Daddy, and then Mommy's gotta go to work." I follow her into the kitchen, setting the remaining coffees and pastries on the table. As I expected, Cole has his hands full with Cassidy, so I hold out my arms to take the baby from Blaire. Melody immediately reaches for my hair, and I indulge her in one tug before gently prying her fingers free.

Blaire's snooping in the bag I set down. "I thought you were leaving?" I say.

She pulls her hand out, her pastry claimed. "I am. I'm outta here. Love you, bye!" She leans over to give Cole a peck, and she's off like a blur of Christmas lights.

Cole holds Cassidy against his body and pulls the drink holder to him, pulling out his flat white, extra cinnamon. He raises an eyebrow as he takes a sip and waits.

I sit down in the chair across from him and mimic his pose with Melody. "So, what do you want to know?"

"*So*, what is there to know?" he responds.

"Well, the pipes burst above . . ."

"Yeah, yeah. I want to know the things I haven't heard from three different townspeople on one trip to the store for diapers. Give me the good stuff."

"Again with the gossip," I say, sipping my own coffee, a ginger-bread latte. Brody says it's one of his favorites so far, and I wanted to try it for myself.

"I'm not allowed to listen to my true crime podcasts anymore because I'm afraid of what I'll miss wearing headphones, and Blaire says we're not raising the girls in a murder house. I'll take my titillation where I can get it. Go."

I let out a sigh, feeling a little bit bad I'm giving him such a hard time when this is what I came here for. "Well, it all started after decoration shopping with some mistletoe."

Cole listens, not interrupting as I detail my reaction to the mistletoe, Brody's proposition, our shower activities, and putting him to bed last night.

"I can't decide if this is better or worse than I expected," he says, pulling a toy out of thin air to distract Cassidy, who is starting to fuss in his arms. Her sister got antsy during my story time, so I shifted so her head is on my shoulder. If the wet spot near my collar is any indication, she's passed out.

"You expected us to have sex?"

Cole levels his eyes at me.

"I'm not *that* fucking predictable," I mutter, wincing as I once again dread the not-so-distant future when I won't be able to get away with that kind of language.

His eyes soften immediately. "Oh Austin, I didn't mean that at all. I'm pretty sure Brody's the only person you've ever loved in a romantic way. So, I'm not surprised you're trying to express those emotions in a way you're more comfortable with."

I slump further in the chair, careful not to jostle the sleeping angel in my arms. "So I am a slut. Kidding!" I say when Cole throws a napkin at me across the table. "You may have a point. I tend to keep things physical and not let anyone get too close."

"So, is Brody too close?" Cole asks, raising his eyebrow again.

"What do you think?"

"I think you need to stop deflecting."

I sigh but then remember I wanted this conversation. No, I need it. "I think even when I had no idea where he was, he was too close."

"What are you going to do?" he asks, gesturing for me to follow him into the living room so we can lay the girls in their bassinets, Cassidy finally having fallen asleep too.

"Is it selfish to want to have him this way?"

"You said keeping things physical was his idea. You don't believe he means it?"

I shrug. "I think he wants to mean it. He says he hasn't had a real relationship since we broke up either, so I do believe he has more experience separating emotion from sex. But whether he can do it when it's between us? Part of me hates the idea that he can."

"But can you? You know I don't want you to get hurt."

I shrug again, missing the weight of a baby keeping my shoulders still, stopping me from being so uncommitted. "I've gotten pretty good at lying to myself when I need to over the years. But even I can't buy into the thought that it won't hurt when he leaves either way. So if he wants to give me, give us, this time, why not take it?"

Cole sighs. "Well then, I guess you better bring him over with you for dinner on Sunday night." He reads my incredulous look dead on. "What? I promise I'll be good!"

Chapter 16

Brody

My body is stiff from moving so little in my sleep last night. I blink against the bright light coming through the blinds. For the second day in a row, it's much later than I usually start the day. I wonder if I can replicate anything else for the second day in a row?

The thought has me sitting up in bed, ready to go searching for my caretaker. My lips turn up when I remember how he feathered the softest kiss on my forehead. My smile grows when I spot the suit I haphazardly left lying on the floor in the haze of pain hanging in the closet. That man doesn't give himself enough credit for how thoughtful he is.

Speaking of which, I pull my hand away from stretching out my back to find it covered in chocolate. A glance behind me finds melted chocolate all over the sheets, too. Well, guess laundry needs to be on the docket for this morning too.

Standing slowly, the medicine sometimes having a woozy aftereffect, I gather my bearings and then strip the bed. The scent of freshly brewed coffee wafts in from the kitchen, and my stomach growls. I haven't had anything to eat since lunchtime yesterday, which may have contributed to how bad the headache got once it started and definitely explains how hungry I am now.

With sheets in hand, I head to the kitchen expecting to find Austin on the couch or at the table. I don't find him in either place, but continue my path to the washing machine to get the sheets started. Cup of coffee poured, I take a sip before listening to the quiet of the apartment. Both of the doors to his bedroom and the bathroom are open—where is he? On my way to investigate, a piece of paper on the table catches my eye. A few steps closer and I recognize Austin's handwriting and his car keys.

I read the note quickly, a twisting feeling in my gut. He's right on when he knew I'd worry to wake up and find him not here. I also can't help but notice he didn't say everything would be okay.

A quick check of the clock shows it's almost ten. I don't want to cut it close two days in a row. The faster I get ready and get to the gym, the sooner I'll see Austin and get a read on where his head's at. A few deep breaths and positive intentions later, I get into motion.

After a shower and a quick egg scramble, I'm ready to hit the road. It's been a long time since I've been behind the wheel of a car, but traffic is light in the pre-lunch hour, and I make it to the gym faster than I expect. With some time to kill before I go inside, I decide to give my Grandma a call.

"How's my favorite Santa grandson?" she answers in lieu of a greeting.

"Last I checked, I'm your only grandson, let alone the only grandchild who plays Santa."

"*Psh*, don't sass me, boy. And since you asked, I'm fine. The cold spell last week brought out the ache in my hip, but nothing a little hot water bottle and that nice masseuse from the spa can't fix." I shake my head even though she can't see me, knowing a request to not overshare would be met with even more details. To think I almost missed out on what's become one of the most important relationships in my life.

"Sorry, Grams. I'm okay. Things are good here. We've been able to connect with a lot of new families, and we're going to make some really great Christmases happen for these folks."

She claps her hands, letting me know I'm on speaker. Now that I know to listen for it, I hear the slow whir of her treadmill. I'm relieved to know her hip really is doing better.

"That's so wonderful, Brody. I'm so proud of you. And how about that beau of yours?"

If you had told me when I moved to NYC and reconnected with the grandma, who'd been absent most of my life, that ten years later she'd be my closest confidante, I wouldn't have believed you. "He's not my beau, Grams." I ignore the *psh* noise she makes and keep going. "But I did need to move in with him because the pipes burst in the place I was staying."

The sound of her hand slamming on the emergency stop button rings through the receiver. "Why are you letting me talk about my hip like some old woman when you've been holding out on real news?"

I laugh. "I don't know. He's still pretty wary of trusting me. I told him what happened and why I left—and I think I've managed to convince him it's not because I've ever been in any way ashamed of him."

"Well, does he know the rest?" My silence answers for me. "Brody Alexander Walker. Why you left is important to who you were, but what happened four years ago is who you *are*. You can't expect him to let you in if he doesn't know the true heart of you."

She's right. I know she is. "I'll . . . I'll try to tell him tonight."

"Do better than try, young man. And be sure to let me know when you'll be back in town for our next dinner and if I'll need to set a third place for your young man."

My heart aches, both in missing her, but also at what being back with her for dinners means. When I'm back to my normal life, my time in Winterberry Glen, and with Austin, will be over. She may think there will be a reason for them to meet, but I'm not so sure.

"I will, Grams. I better go get changed for today's Santa time."

"Go make some days, Grandson. I love you."

"I love you, too."

My heart is lighter than it has been in days, and my resolve is stronger too. Whether Austin wants to keep things platonic, or is willing to explore more, he deserves to know me. The me I am now.

I walk into the locker room and find Austin sitting on the bench, hair wet and tights already in place.

"Austin," I say, surprised he snuck past me in the parking lot.

"I saw you were on the phone, so I didn't stop to say hi. Everything okay?"

His expression is unreadable. I wish he'd give me *something*.

"I dunno. Is everything okay?"

He pushes to his feet, and I stand my ground as he walks toward me, stopping inches away. Our eyes lock, and whatever he sees in mine makes him smile.

"I think it will be," he says, before leaning in to kiss me. He takes the opportunity to bite my bottom lip lightly before pulling away. The mirth in his eyes is worth all the worry this morning.

"Let's go, Santa. We've got ourselves a full slate today. Plus, we need to go pick up those coffees you promised everyone." He smacks my ass and moves around me to the bathroom stalls.

I won't have to try very hard to be a right jolly old elf today.

Turns out, staying jolly is much harder than I expected. At least once every season there's a day where nothing goes right. Tantrums galore, tech issues, impatient crowds, short staffed— you name it, we had it. The hushed air when the door closes after the last family is heavy with exhaustion and frustration.

I wipe my face and decide I need to say something. "Hey everyone, give me a minute?" All the elves drop whatever closing up activity they were half-heartedly going through the motions of, and gather around, standing among the line stanchions. Jasmine even sinks to the floor, leaning against a particularly large present box.

"In the Santa biz, we call days like today a dark day. You all did your very best to keep up with everything the day threw at us, and I'll be sure to tell Blaire the same thing. I wish I could say we've had our fill and it won't happen again, but the closer we get to Christmas, the higher tensions rise. Hopefully, they will be isolated incidents, but remember why we're here. To put smiles on those kids' faces, whether their parents appreciate it or not. Let's clean up as quickly as we can, go home, and get some rest. Breakfast and lunch are on me tomorrow."

A few scattered claps ring out. Everyone gets back to their assignments with a bit more pep in their step—exhausted pep, but still.

I pull out my phone. Before I can start putting anything into action, Austin steps up next to me. "Are all Santas this good at rallying the troops?" he asks, leaning casually against the side of my chair. My face reddens.

"Maybe not all of them, but the ones who care about the people they're working with should be." The look in his eyes shows he's impressed, and it's hard for me to hold his gaze. I look back at my phone instead, typing fast and furious.

"So how are you going to get breakfast and lunch organized that quickly? Need me to make some calls?" he asks.

"Thanks, but I got it. Susie and I set up an emergency plan—and an emergency account—on my second day here. I wish it weren't the turn from weekday to weekend hours, but she'll get it done." Right on cue, she texts back "10-4," and I know there will be even more than I requested waiting for us to pick up in the morning.

"You can text Blaire now, but if you want a chance to fill her in more, you could do it at dinner on Sunday night," he says casually. I look up from my phone in a flash. Austin's face betrays the nerves his voice hid.

"Dinner with Blaire . . . does that mean dinner with Cole too?" I ask, wary. The fierce friend I know Cole can be, I'm not sure how Austin's breakfast went this morning. Though his kiss in the locker room may be a clue.

"Mmhm." Austin nods. "It was his idea to bring you, actually."

I raise an eyebrow.

"Not that I don't want you there, really. The good idea was probably inspired by my presence. But"—his expression turns serious—"I'd really like you to be there."

"Nice save," I say, smacking his arm gently. "Now, go get moving on your cleanup. No special treatment from Santa in the workshop."

"So there is the potential for *special* treatment," he says, his voice all innuendo. I look around, and catch Jimmy watching us, but everyone else is hustling. Jimmy rolls his eyes, but softens it with a smile before unplugging the computer and waving good-bye. I know he'll be up late cleaning the database, making sure the bright spots from today—the people we're going to help—don't get overshadowed by the tough cases.

"Only for the really *good* boys," I say, my voice low and husky.

Austin salutes and saunters away. I can't help but reflect on how good it feels to have someone to joke around with after a hard day like the one we had today. To know I'm not going home by myself, even if I'm not quite sure *what* it is I'm going home to, means even more that it's Austin I'm sharing it with. And I plan to hold on to this feeling, for however long I have it.

"I know I've only been an elf for about two weeks, but I thought it would be more toy making and less exhausting," Austin says, flopping onto the couch after we get back to his place. "Home" he called it again as we were leaving. It's hard not to read too much into his words. It is his home. Does he want me to view it as a place to call home too?

"Well, you know, even toy making can be grueling. After all,

Ming-Ming expected a thousand Etch-A-Sketches a day," I say, knowing he'll get the reference immediately.

"Fuck, now I want to watch *Elf*, but considering we need to be back at the workshop in less than twelve hours, it's probably not the responsible thing to do."

"Rain check." I roll my neck along the back of the couch to look at him.

"Snowball check," he responds, mimicking my pose and giving me a happy look, not unlike the one he probably sees on my face.

"So, I guess we should go to bed then." There's a question, an invitation there, and I think back to my conversation with Grams this morning. Some combo of grandmotherly thoughts and bed tickles my memory . . .

"Fuck," I exclaim, sitting straight up. "My sheets are still in the washer from this morning."

"Oh, they are, are they?" Austin looks amused. "How convenient. Did you know I only have the one set of sheets for your bed?"

"Stop." I laugh through my words. "This is actually your fault. I fell asleep with chocolate in my bed last night, which wouldn't have happened without you bringing it to me."

"So sorry for caring," he says, and the mood sobers slightly. "Well, you can kick it on the couch until they finish, or . . ."

I try not to show my excitement. "Or?"

"I do know another place you could sleep," he says. His look of one is resolve and certainty. What the hell happened during his conversation with Cole today?

"Do you now?" I respond. We sit in silence for a beat or two. "I'm going to need you to actually say it, Austin."

"Come to bed, Brody." He pushes off the couch and walks to the bathroom without looking back.

How can I refuse an offer like that?

I'm in my room getting ready for bed when he heads into to

his room. After a quick trip of my own to the bathroom, I take a deep breath and head for his doorway.

The sight in front of me stops me in my tracks. Austin's sitting up in bed, shirtless, his defined chest and abs on full display. The blankets are pooled around his lap, and a pair of glasses sit on his nose as he looks at his phone.

Squeaky floorboard strikes again and announces my presence. He looks up and meets my gaze.

"Glasses, really?" I ask, crossing the room and climbing into bed on the side he's left empty for me. It seems easier to harp on the frames resting on his nose than think too hard about the fact I'm climbing back into bed with Austin Owens.

He smirks. "Do something for you?" He takes them off and sets them on the nightstand. "They're for reading—my eyes are more tired at night, so I can get away without them most of the time."

"I'll speak on behalf of humankind to say we would be okay with it if you couldn't."

Austin laughs and leans toward me, cupping my face in his hand. He brings his lips to mine, and my eyes flutter shut. His lips are soft and tender, a kiss full of greeting and full of relief, like coming back home after a long time away.

He pulls away a few inches but keeps his hand on my face. "So," he starts.

"So," I respond, wondering if he feels the familiarity I do.

"I would like to formally accept your offer. Just sex. With our expiration date, I think it's best."

I wince at the honesty in his words, even though they were my idea. He smiles kindly, stroking my beard with his thumb.

"What do you think?" His eyes search mine.

"Before I can accept your acceptance"—I swallow past a lump in my throat—"I want to tell you why I'm not a lawyer anymore."

He sits back. "Tonight?"

I nod. "It's important to me you know everything before anything else happens between us." I move my hand back and forth between us, like he could really think I was referring to anyone else.

"Okay, I'm listening." He shifts slightly so his body is inclined toward mine, settling against his pillows.

"Need a cup of coffee? It's a long story." I laugh, nervous to share the story with someone who knew me before and someone I want to know me after.

He doesn't respond, but reaches out and takes my hand, tangling my fingers with his. My focus stays there while I start talking.

"My entire life, I'd been on a course, a plan. Pre-law in college, so I could get an idea of what type of law I wanted to practice, experience as a paralegal for a few years, and then law school. Become a lawyer like my dad, and his dad before him, and his dad before him. Only, no one else's dad took the plan quite so seriously. He and his mom had a falling out not long after I was born. Looking back now, with the lens of some therapy, it's pretty clear he projected his emotions from processing his hurt onto me and my future. Dad never came out explicitly and said if I didn't follow the plan, I could risk falling into the same fate of losing my family, but the implications were pretty clear.

"Me coming to Winterberry Glen at all was an adjustment of the plan. But Todd Johnson is one of the best in Mergers and Acquisitions to this day. Dad was thrilled, and even at twenty-four, his approval meant everything. Then came you. The brightest bright spot I never knew was missing. Dating went expressly against the plan. I know you think I couldn't tell you were interested. I tried to stay away. But I couldn't. And then I made the biggest mistake of all. I fell in love with you."

His hand squeezes mine. How he knows I need that grounding to go on, well, I shouldn't be surprised by now. I squeeze back knowing this next part is going to be tough.

"Fast forward to the summer I'm supposed to leave for law school. I've decided on MassU, we're going to be able to make this work. And then I get the news they've pulled my funding. *The plan* dictates we're supposed to be fully funded and not go into debt. Everything coming so close to falling apart, it felt like life was getting back at me for trying to have it all. The extended time before law school, you. I had to give something up. Except it's weeks before the semester is supposed to start and I'm out of options.

"I go for a Hail Mary. Looking back, that call may have been the beginning of the end of the plan, even though it would take another six years to fully leave it. I call my grandma. The same one my dad hasn't spoken to in decades. NYU reached out to me once they saw my name on the LSAT lists, so I knew she still had connections. Turns out, connected is an understatement. The Walkers have a conference room, a lecture hall, and a student lounge in the law school. Grandma agrees to make a call, on one condition."

"What was it?" Austin asks. His attention hasn't wavered in the slightest, even when I describe my cowardice in believing in the realness of what we had.

I laugh then. "Well, one of "the girls" at Gram's DAR chapter had given her the scoop on a little show called *Gilmore Girls*. Grandma decided to channel her inner Emily Gilmore and required my presence at weekly dinners in exchange for calling in this favor. Too good a deal to pass up, I agreed and left for New York the next day." It's my turn to squeeze his hand in apology. He squeezes back, nodding for me to continue.

"Suddenly, the family matriarch I thought had cut us all off is the person I see most outside of law school other than the Starbucks barista on the way to campus. The one thing we don't talk about is why my dad stopped talking to her, but we talked about anything and everything else. She and grandpa met at NYU Law, you see—a part of the family history my dad conveniently left out. Gramps died before I was born—around the time my dad blew up his relationship with his mom."

"Did she ever tell you what happened?"

I nod. "She did. I'll get to that, I promise. So, law school is over, I'm hired by a major firm, living and working in Manhattan, making disgusting amounts of money. By all intents and purposes, the plan has been a rousing success . . ." I trail off there, thinking about my mental state at the time. The lowest I've ever been and hopefully the lowest I'll ever be.

"But you weren't happy?" Austin fills in the rest of the sentence. My response is a sad smile.

"Absolutely miserable. Barely eating or sleeping, working fourteen-hour days, having panic attacks in my office, avoiding Grams, because she put my dad on this same plan—what would she say if she saw how much I struggled, how I wasted the faith she had in me."

"Oh, Brody," he says, like I'm breaking his heart all over again.

I swallow. "I know. I was pretty lost. But then one day, I have to pull over at a community center to use the bathroom on the way home from a deposition upstate—drinking too much caffeine also didn't help my anxiety or lack of sleep. On my way to the bathroom, I pass an open door, with a sign out front that says 'Professional Santa School.' My instinct was to roll my eyes, but I had to walk past them again to get back to my car. I stopped to listen and realized it was an open-house-orientation-type event. And for the first time in three years, I didn't think about my time in six-minute increments. I walked into the classroom, sat down, and listened. These guys were legit and put so much passion and investment into their work. But instead of greed, their work was spreading joy. Before I knew it, I had been there the better part of an hour. I had a meeting in thirty minutes and was still forty-five minutes outside of the city. The panic started to come back, so I left without talking to anyone. But luckily, I grabbed one of their cards.

"I drove back to the city in a state—I still don't remember it very well. But instead of driving to the office, I drove to my grandma's place on Central Park West. I'd been dodging her calls for months, but she never took me off the approved visitor's list. She answered the door herself, on her way out to play pickleball, I think. She took one look at my face, opened her arms, and I fell into them."

My voice cracks at the memory of that breakdown. Austin scoots the rest of the way to me, and tucks his head onto my shoulder, a perfect fit. He wraps his arms around my middle. "Sorry," he says. "I can give you space, but I thought I might break apart if I couldn't hug you."

I press a kiss to the top of his head, and wrap an arm around his shoulders, caressing his arm. "I'll always take a hug from you."

"So, you quit being a lawyer to be Santa?" he asks, his words muffled into my neck.

"Not at first," I say. "First, I quit being a lawyer to get healthy. Grams insisted I move in—said she had the space, and she's not wrong." Austin laughs, and the mood lifts somewhat. "I started therapy, got a nutritionist, signed up for yoga classes. I know I'm lucky I had somewhere safe to go, with someone who was willing to share all they had with me to help me get better. I let go of the plan, those 4:00 a.m. gym workouts and limited eating to maintain a body type I thought a corporate lawyer should have. And then, after a few months, yes, I enrolled in Santa school."

Austin tickles my stomach. "It's like you were made to play the role. It allows you to be who you are."

My heart expands so much it might burst. Grandma's going to crow when I tell her she's right—it does feel so good to have someone see me for who I am.

"The Santa Squad—what the teachers call themselves—did say I'm a natural. So much of a natural, they said I shouldn't be working for someone else but should have my pick of gigs. And I'll admit, my brain did miss planning and strategizing and working toward a goal. I decided to create my own business."

He sits back up so he can look me in the eye, pulling my legs so they're tangled with his. Our shoulders rest against one another. "So then the philanthropy part. How did you decide to expand beyond Santa appearances?"

I smile. "Ah, that's all grandma. I told her about my idea to start a business. I had a decent amount of savings and investments, which were growing well by staying with her. She reminded me of what I thought the first time I saw the Santas. How their passion and energy is directed toward helping others, not toward helping themselves. What would I do to keep that in my business?"

"And so Scott's Tots was born." I shove him, and we both laugh.

"It's called Holidays with Margot, after the inspiration herself. And honestly, she's the only reason it's happened and I can keep doing this."

"I do have to admit, I wondered how being Santa six weeks a year made enough to live the other forty-six weeks."

"There are a surprising number of random one-offs during the rest of the year. But after we hashed out the idea for the charitable part of the business, she told me what happened with my dad. After my grandpa died, Grams reevaluated a lot of parts of her life. Lots of therapy and reflection of her own. She realized they had pushed my dad incredibly hard, probably too hard. And she did not want him to do the same to me. He took it personally to his core, thought it meant they were disappointed in him when all he'd done was meet their standards and goalposts his entire life. He wouldn't listen when she said that wasn't true and cut her off. If anything, he increased the pressure on the plan for me.

"Grandma said she couldn't get through to him, but I had found the same truth she did. Focusing on what you can do for others, rather than what you can do for yourself, is far more enriching. So, she gave me my inheritance early—a house in Stamford, investments, and liquid assets. Enough so I'd never have to work another day in my life if I didn't want to, but if anything, it only made me work harder to get the business off the ground, to help as many people as I can. I don't think I've made a business decision with myself as the focus until Blaire called and offered me the chance to come back. To come back to you."

We sit in silence then, both staring into space. I don't think

I've talked this long, all at once, since my last trial. There's been a lot of self-work and change in the past four years. I'll give Austin all the time he needs to process.

"Thank you for telling me," he says, turning his face to mine.

"Thank you for listening." And for the first time in ten years, I'm the one to bring my lips to meet Austin's, initiating a kiss, long and slow.

"Not sure how anyone could consider Santa a sexless figure after hearing your story—self-awareness and philanthropy is hot," he says against my lips, and we laugh into each other's mouths.

I pull back and run my fingers through his hair. "I'm not sure many people see Santa Brody quite the same way you do."

He shrugs. "Probably for the best." The end of his sentence is interrupted by a yawn, and I see it's almost midnight.

Like he reads my mind. "But we'll have to save all the Santa sexiness for another time. Can't have Santa falling asleep on the job because his elf rocked his world too hard." He reaches to turn off the light on his side of the bed.

We both snuggle into the sheets and face each other. Austin smiles a sleepy smile and pushes on my shoulder so I roll over. He molds himself to my back, lacing our hands together in front of my chest. I hug his arm to me with both of mine. It's as if I'm already dreaming, getting to be back in Austin's arms.

"Night, Santa," he murmurs into my hair. His breathing evens out almost immediately and I allow myself to lulled by the rhythm of it, his heat against my back.

"You're the only present I ever need," I whisper into the darkness, before I follow him into sugarplum dreams.

Chapter 17

Austin

The alarm sounds, breaking up one of the best nights of sleep I've had in a long time. *Maybe a decade*, I think, as Brody shifts behind me, our positions swapping at some point in the night.

"I don't want to be Santa today," Brody says into the nape of my neck, before sitting upright. "I didn't mean it. I love being Santa." I roll over to see his eyes open in shock and have to bite my lip not to laugh at him.

"You can love being Santa and wish for a little more time to snuggle in bed. I know I do." I put my hand on his leg where it's covered by the sheet. I don't trust myself to touch his bare skin right now, especially while he's already having a crisis of conscience.

He nods, a solemn look on his face, saying, "You're right," before scrubbing any remaining sleep from his eyes.

"You go shower," I say, swinging my legs off the bed and wandering to the dresser for a pair of flannel pants. "I'll make breakfast." I turn around to see Brody's eyes locked on where my ass, and now my junk, are disappearing into blue and black plaid. "Brody. Santa time. And we have to swing by Jitters to pick everything up before we change."

"Right." He visibly shakes himself. "You have more willpower than I do."

I stalk over to the bed, putting one knee between where his legs are spread, bringing my face inches from his. "Or more of an appreciation for delayed gratification." He leans forward chasing my mouth, but I pull back before he can make contact.

"I'm putting you on the naughty list," he groans.

I walk away, laughing. "Oh baby, I'm already there." With a wink over my shoulder, I head to the kitchen to make us something to eat, first breakfast if you will. I think we'll need our energy today.

You'd think everyone working at the workshop today spent the night snuggling with their ex, the way we're hustling and humming along. I worried a dip in energy would follow yesterday's rough ending, but never underestimate the power of a good leader and free pastries and coffee. We book out more slots on these weekend days in December, but somehow, we're keeping right on schedule.

Jimmy is getting information from almost everyone who comes through—he presented Brody with the idea to gather information from everyone, regardless of need. He pointed out that it makes things slightly less conspicuous for those who want to keep a low profile. It also allows those who may be able to help this year to receive information about donating to the future of Brody's cause. I thought Brody might kiss him, saying how this would change the trajectory of who he could help and how. But nope, those lips are only for me.

I manage to keep finding reasons to touch Brody, innocently, of course. As Santa and his elf. Whether it's bringing Santa a refill for his water, or being extra cautious in the handoff of his visitors, every brush of his hand sends sparks shooting through me. I don't know what my plans for Brody tonight will contain, but I know they're going to be big, long, and hard.

A throat clears next to me, and Brody shoots me a knowing look. Seems my eyes are getting a little too lusty. I need to lock it down for a little while longer. I groan internally with a glance at the clock on the wall. Okay, so several more hours longer.

As the afternoon wears on, I start to notice that more than the children visiting are appreciating Santa Brody. Single parents of all varieties are giving him heart eyes, and it's getting my tinsel in a tangle. Have they been looking at him like this all along, and I've been too busy trying to *stop* myself from looking to notice?

It doesn't matter. Brody hasn't touched a woman romantically since the tenth grade homecoming dance. These women are not being subtle in their appreciation for how they think Brody could drive their sleigh. It seems to me like even the dads are hitting on him.

One steps in front the elf taking photos. "Wait, sweetie, you wanted to hold your Rudolph stuffy in your picture with Santa." He steps forward, handing the reindeer over. Leaning closer to Brody than I think entirely necessary, he hums. "Wow, Santa, that's some nice cologne you have on there. What's it called? I'd love to put it on my Christmas list." It's all too much, and suddenly I'm seeing red.

"Excuse me," I say, stepping up, my voice more abominable snowman than human. I take a breath. "If you can step behind the rope, we need to keep the line moving." I stand between him and the camera while the photographer finishes up, and Brody's eyes stay on me, dancing with humor.

"Careful, Austin. Elves don't growl," he whispers when I step forward to help the little girl back to her overly flirtatious father.

"They might if they were the ones sleeping with Santa instead of Mrs. Claus," I mutter back.

And that's how I know I've been spending too many hours in the North Pole—all my metaphors are coming out Christmassy.

Around 3:30 p.m., there's a commotion at the door. The

college girls working at the door today start to look panicked, and Brody nods when I ask with my eyes if I should go help.

"I don't care if I booked for tomorrow. I thought today was the ninth. We drove the whole way here, and you need to let me in." The woman tries to bullrush the door and looks up in surprise when I don't budge. "Excuse me, let me in."

"Ma'am, I understand you're frustrated, but all the people in front of you and the sizable crowd now waiting behind you in the cold have reservations for today," I say. My eyes look with purpose at the line of people behind her. She turns her head, and when she looks back, her cheeks are red—whether with embarrassment, renewed purpose, or anger, I'm not sure.

"I've never been treated this way in all my life," she shouts, bringing the rest of the noise in the workshop to a stop for a second until an enterprising elf starts a sing-a-long of Jingle Bells to distract the kids in line. Renewed angry purpose, it is. "How can you keep kids from seeing Santa?" The kids in question are tugging on her hand. Even under the age of eight, they know Mom's wrong.

"If you had explained the situation to my co-elves here, we would have been happy to see if we have space in the next little while for you." I let my voice convey how her demanding to see Santa on a day when she doesn't have a booking sounds about as ludicrous as being angry we don't have a real life Rudolph to take people on flights in the sky. "But as it stands, we'll be refunding your booking for tomorrow. Have a great day."

I stand there with my arms crossed, waiting for her to turn and leave.

"I'll blast this festival! I'll ruin you . . ." Her voice wavers as she realizes people around us are recording.

"My boss probably wouldn't love it if we went viral for the wrong reasons, but seeing as you forced your way into the workshop, and you signed a release saying you understood the risk of being photographed or recorded on official festival grounds when you booked your tickets, we can release any of these videos to the press and be sure the real story gets out."

Jimmy appears at my side then, a cookie bag in each hand. As the woman storms away, leaving her children behind to follow, he stops the older one. "Allergies?" he asks, and she shakes her head no, not able to meet his eyes. Poor kids. Jimmy hands them each a cookie. "Merry Christmas," he says, and they walk away hand in hand, their mother waiting for them twenty-five yards away from the door.

"Sorry about the delay, folks," I say to everyone outside moving forward to check in now. Luckily, the overall atmosphere seems to be understanding. Before going back to my post next to Brody, I hide behind the false wall for a second and give Blaire a heads up. Her GIF response of George Michael from *Arrested Development* laying down on the carpet tells me everything I need to know about how her day is going.

Back at the Santa station, a mom is standing off to the side, waiting for her son to finish with Brody. She looks vaguely familiar, like I've seen her around Winterberry Glen. Two more steps has her right next to me.

"Some people have all the nerve," she says. "You handled her really well. I'm Victoria. You're Austin, right?" I take her outstretched hand.

"Yeah, I'm sorry, do I—"

"Oh, no. I've seen you around, though. Never had a chance to say hi before." She puts her hand on my arm then and leaves it. "So, hi."

A throat clears to our left, and I find Brody, looking much more murderous than Santa ever should. It's pretty fucking sexy. "Excuse me, ma'am? Lillian needs to use the bathroom."

"Duty calls," she says. "Maybe I'll see you around sometime."

"Merry Christmas," I say in response, biting back a smile as the pair walks away. I walk to Brody under the guise of handing him his water bottle. "Needed to pee, huh?" I ask under my breath.

He takes a gulp of water first. "What, she's four, and this line is at least thirty minutes long. There's a good chance she does," he says, no shame in his voice.

"Careful, Brody. Santa doesn't growl," I echo back, leaning down to set his bottle on the ground.

"Under the right circumstances, this Santa might," he breathes, before exclaiming, "Ho, Ho, Ho!" in greeting to his next visitor.

Five p.m. has never been so far away.

We're down to the last family, and it's clear this child has had too much time to think about sitting in a stranger's lap and probably missed an afternoon nap. After Dad sets him in Brody's lap, the kid looks into his face and starts to sob. I've seen Brody work some magic on criers over the past couple of weeks, but this one's worked up a full head of steam, and I'm unsure. Still, Brody holds his hand up to Dad, asking him to give them a second.

"Hey there. It's okay. I know meeting new people can be hard." The kid nods through his tears, and again somehow, Brody hit right on what this child is struggling with. "I get scared sometimes, too. But I know finding something in common can help them feel a little more familiar. Tell me." He pauses, looking up at Dad for a little help with the name. "Austin," Dad mouths. Brody has to work not to laugh.

"Tell me, Austin, what's your favorite Christmas carol?"

Austin whimpers but doesn't say anything. Dad looks about ready to call it quits, but something in me wants to help this kindred Austin be brave. I take a step up and kneel next to Brody's chair.

"Hi, Austin. What a great name. It's my name too!" He sniffs and opens his eyes wide, his lip trembling like it wants to smile. "My favorite Christmas carol is Frosty."

"Swanta Cwaus," he mumbles, and Brody's face breaks into a huge smile.

"Santa Claus is Coming to Town?" Brody asks, and little Austin nods, wiping his eye. "That's my favorite, too. It talks about how I get to go to towns like this one and meet people like you."

Austin breaks into a true smile then, his eyes still wet and red, but the tears have passed. His little hand grabs onto Brody's, and he reaches across Brody's lap to tug on my fingers from where they rest on the chair's arm. I let him pull my hand closer to his body and exchange a look with Brody telling me I'm not the only one experiencing a storm of emotions. Working together to connect with this kid, have him accept us both, it's overwhelming.

Brody recovers first. "So, Austin, what do you want for Christmas?"

"A puppy and a scooter," he says matter-of-factly, nodding in satisfaction he got the job done. A look at the mirth on Dad's face tells me they've been practicing.

"Well, all right, Austin, I'll see what I can do. Thanks for coming to see me and Austin today. My friend Jimmy over there has a cookie for you, if Dad says it's okay."

Austin lets go of our hands and holds his out for Dad, who walks over and gathers him up in his arms. "Thanks, guys, you were great with him. If you all ever get lost delivering presents on Christmas Eve, you can always crash at our place." With his voice full of innuendo, he gives us a wink, and thank goodness little Austin is too busy straining for his cookie to overhear. I wouldn't want to have to explain to a three-year-old Santa won't actually be coming by for a sleepover.

Brody blinks at me, not quite sure how to react, and I laugh, putting my head down on top his arm where it rests on the arm of the chair. "Not into the group thing, then?" I ask him.

He shakes his head. "No, I've never . . . wait, have you?" I shrug, this not even being close to the place to get into it. His head shakes again. "Never mind, I don't want to know. But no, I *don't* share."

The possessiveness in his voice, added with watching people want what's mine all day, snaps something in me. I don't want to wait, *can't* wait until we get home. A memory of something we did ten years ago—and the somewhere we did it—flashes through my mind. I know what to do next.

"Follow my lead, okay?" I say quietly, and Brody sends me a questioning look.

"Hey everyone, y'all can head out early. Blaire needs to take some promo photos of Brody and wants the space clear to do it. We'll clean everything up." No one needs to be told twice to pack up and head home, and most rush out like I might take it back if they stay behind.

"Liar, liar, tights on fire," Jimmy says as he saunters past me. "Just remember, this place will be crawling with kids again in the morning."

"Night, Jimmy," I say. That kid doesn't miss anything.

I lock the back door behind him, and come out to find Brody standing in front of his chair.

"Sit," I say when I walk past. He drops back into the chair. "Blaire wants to do promo photos tonight? Wouldn't it be better with some natural light?" The lock on the front door clicks into place as I turn and walk back toward him with intent.

"Oh," he says, and I watch his throat bob as he swallows hard. "Blaire's not taking any pictures, is she?"

"Nope," I say, enunciating the "P" as I come to a stop in front of him. With an arm braced on each side of his chair, I lean down. "So, why don't you tell me again about how Santa's basically a sexless figure?"

"What? He is. No one wants to have sex with Santa."

I scoff. "Please. Tell that to all the parents who hit on you today. I think some people without kids came along with friends to get a look."

His eyes roll. "That's a bit much. Some people are committed aunties and uncles." He inhales sharply when I trail my nose from the base of his neck up to his ear.

"You don't see what I see," I say into his ear, my voice low and serious.

"What do you see?" he asks, tipping his head back, easing my path back down his cheek, under his chin, and up to the other ear. Once there, I answer him. "A sexy man who doesn't realize the spell he casts on people. Who cares so fucking much it drives me insane. Who can make me feel paternal one second and then horny as hell as soon as the child walks away." I bite down on his earlobe and he groans. His hands come in to grip my hips, tugging me back slightly so he can see my face.

"Well, how about what I see?"

I raise my eyebrow, feeling cocky, until he stretches to place a kiss where it's arched. My breath stutters when he starts to speak. "I see a man tempting me to get coal in my stocking for the rest of my life. The thoughts he puts into my head with his ass in those tights." His lips move across my forehead, then trail down to the side of my mouth. "Who stands up for what's right, for those he cares about. Who helped a little boy feel comfortable with a stranger. Who is the only one this Santa wants." He says those last words against my mouth, and I crash into him.

His back hits the back of his chair, and I thank whoever designs Santa thrones for their roomy nature as I straddle his legs. My hand seeks his hair to tangle in, knocking his red cap askew. My tight grip on the strands lets me angle his head how I want it to ravage his mouth. I bear down all my weight onto his lap, and his groan fills my mouth when I grind on his dick. A slow, firm circle of my hips has me swallowing that noise over and over.

He yanks his mouth away from mine. "Austin, I cannot take these pants to the dry cleaner to get cum out of them."

"Buy new ones," I say, diving back in for a kiss. A grip on my hair pulls me back again.

"They're custom made." His eyes are playful, a wanting as strong as mine behind the mirth. It wouldn't be fun if it were easy.

"Aren't you supposed to be rich?" I ask, already removing my weight from his lap, leaning back to get a better look at him. His lips are as red as his suit, and his hair is absolutely wrecked. The swells of his cheeks are deliciously rosy, both from the kisses and the heat of our bodies in his velvet suit.

"But not wasteful," he says, even as he tries to pull my face back down to his. He whines in response to me climbing off him.

"Hold your reindeer, Santa," I say, spreading his legs wide so I can kneel between them. "If we can't ruin the pants, then we're just going to have to lose them." My fingers undo the knot on his jacket, opening it enough so I can undo the suspenders holding the pants up. I pause with my fingers in his waistband, looking up at him.

"What?" he asks, his chest heaving in anticipation. He glances around then in a panic. "Did you hear something?"

"No. But I need to . . ." I reach next to him for the Santa hat I knocked off his head earlier and hand it to him to put it back on before curling my finger in the waistband of his red pants again. This time I snag the elastic of his boxer briefs too.

Brody lifts his hips up, helping me work them down below his knees, saying, "Do you have a Santa kink I should know about?"

I lean back to admire my handiwork. Brody's cock is hard against his thigh, a bead of pre-cum at the tip. His white under-shirt has ridden up so a bit of his belly peeks out, while his coat is splayed open. I've never considered if a Santa hat could pull off a "freshly fucked" angle, but we've somehow achieved it. And then there's the face between the hat and coat, pupils dilated, mouth open and panting slightly, breaking up the grey-white beard.

"I think I might be gaining one. Stay still." I push up from the floor and walk to the bathroom.

"Where are you going?" he calls after me.

I'm back a moment later with some paper towels in my hand. "Jimmy has a point. And I intend for things to get a little sloppy." My eyes zero in on where his fist is pumping up and down his length in slow, steady strokes. "I said to stay still."

He shrugs, a cockiness of his own rising on his face. "I felt you left some room for interpretation."

"Lawyers." I set the napkins down and slam to my knees in

front of him. My hand replaces his, my grip tight, causing him to wince before fucking his hips up into my fist.

"Former lawyers," he responds, the word ending in a gasp as I bring my tongue to taste the pre-cum I left waiting, making sure to tongue his slit while I'm there. He looks down his nose at me.

I lick a stripe from the base of his cock to the tip, my hand reaching up to tug on his balls. He gasps, one hand tangling with mine resting on his thigh as his eyes fall closed. He grips tight as I do it again.

"Look at you," I say, my tongue licking a circle around the head of his cock. "They may get you as Santa." I yank his hips forward so his ass is off the front of the chair, putting a crick in his neck to keep his eyes, now open, firmly on me. I stick my finger in my mouth and lick it slowly before running it down his cock, over his balls, and pressing firmly behind his balls. My tongue makes another circle around his cockhead before I speak again. "But no one else gets to see you like this." I swallow his cock next, taking him as far into my throat as I can on one go.

"Ugh," he grunts as I swallow around him.

"Only you," he grits out, the grip on my hand tightening. His other hand grips the arm of the chair so hard I think it might creak.

A few more bobs and I pull off, pleased with the strand of saliva that connects my mouth to his cock when I do. Like I wanted, sloppy.

"That's right. Mine," I say, locking my eyes on his. "Now, I want you to fuck my mouth, Santa. Like you belong on the naughty list too." My gaze never leaves his as I lower my mouth onto him, keeping it loose around his cock, waiting for him to take control.

Brody's hand leaves mine, and he stands up. He towers above me, staring. "God, you look so good on your knees for me."

My cock, which I've done a decent job of ignoring until now, twitches in my tights. His eyes move downward as I pull my shirt up and pull my tights and briefs down until I can grip my cock and give it a few strokes. Brody nods in approval before tangling his hands in my hair. And that's all the warning I get before he pulls his hips back and pistons into my mouth, his cock entering my throat. He sets a quick rhythm, and I kneel there, letting him use my mouth while I stroke myself at the same punishing pace. The hat finally falls off his head with his harsh movements. Both of my hands go to his thighs as he continues to fuck my mouth, my eyes watering. Fuck, I'm closer to the edge than I thought and move on hand to grip the base of my cock tight to stop from decorating the carpet.

"You're. Mine. Too." He grunts before thrusting one last time and holding himself there, filling my throat with his cum. I can't swallow it fast enough, and some dribbles past my lips as he pulls out.

"Where are those napkins?" he asks. I feel around and hand him one. But instead of wiping my face, he sidesteps and kneels next to me. He wipes the saliva and cum off my face and brings his hand to my cock, using the mixture to jack me off. I groan and watch his hand move, right back to the edge again.

"Brody, fuck," I grit out and he gets the napkin up in time, like we're teenagers trying not to stain our sheets. But instead, we're trying not to stain a Santa suit or the carpet in front of Santa's chair.

Once my release is wrapped in another napkin and safely set to the side, Brody sits up on his knees and brings me with him, putting his hand on my face. He leans in and kisses me deeply, mixing the taste of his release with the taste of him. It creates an intoxicating cocktail.

The kiss slows and we part, resting our foreheads together, both breathing deeply.

"Okay, maybe not such a sexless figure, after all," Brody says, and we both laugh. We get ourselves straightened up and finish all the resetting ourselves since I sent everyone away.

I hold out my hand for Brody's once we're done and lead him

out the back door. After it's locked, he starts laughing. "What?" I ask, turning with him, confused.

"So, you know how you said no one else gets to see me that way? What about hearing me?" It takes me a second, but I catch up to his train of thought. The angle of both cameras in the workshop focus on the door and the chair is out of view, thank God. Our eyes meet and I start laughing with him.

"He's going to kill me," I say. "Thank god these feeds aren't monitored live."

"All those five minutes of planning, and you didn't think about the cameras?" Brody teases.

I pull out my phone as we walk back to the high school hand in hand, putting it on speaker.

"Hi, Cole. Listen, I think we need a second dessert for tomorrow night. What are you in the mood for?"

"What did you do?"

"I'm going to need a favor . . ." He sighs multiple times as I explain I need him to wipe the footage from the workshop from the time we closed until now.

"You're lucky I love you. See you tomorrow, Brody," he says, hanging up on me.

"Well, at least now we won't need an icebreaker," I say, and it's his turn to shove me before I wrap him under my arm and press a kiss to the side of his head.

Chapter 18

Brody

Why does walking into dinner with Austin's best friend feel so much harder than staring down 250 kids on a Sunday two weeks before Christmas? Maybe because I know firsthand how easy it is to care about this man and want to hurt anyone who would dare upset him. Myself included.

"You've argued cases in front of judges and juries. This should be easy," Austin says as we walk to Cole and Blaire's front door.

"The stakes weren't as high then," I say, adjusting the bottle of wine, bouquet of flowers, and toys for the girls in my arms. After the camera disaster of last night, I thought it best not to come empty-handed and made Austin take a trip to Doose's on our way back to his place last night.

"Didn't you win several multi-million-dollar settlements?" He reaches his hand out to knock on the door.

"Yeah, I did. Still not as high stakes," I say, distracted by hoping I haven't sweat through the dress shirt under my heavy coat. I'm trying to figure out how to unbutton it to start airing out with my hands full when I realize his hand is still in the air. A glance to my left shows Austin staring at me in surprise. "It's true," I say with a shrug. Austin changes the course of his hand

and wraps it behind my head instead, pulling me in for a kiss. I hold the flowers out to the side of our bodies so they don't get smooshed.

"Ahem." A voice comes from the forgotten doorway of the house we're supposed to be entering. I pull back, and wonder what color on the emergency alert scale my cheeks are right now.

"Hi, Cole," Austin says cheerfully. "Waiting by the door so you can practice your disappointed dad date routine about fifteen years too early?"

The look on our host's face isn't impressed. "Thought I heard a car, so came out to investigate. Glad to see you're still necking in public." He steps back to let us in. "Brody," he says to me, nodding as I walk past. What happens if my face bursts into flames? It'll definitely put a damper on this beard I've worked so hard on.

"Necking, Cole? Seriously?" Blaire stands in the entrance to the living room, her hands on her hips. A peek behind her shows she's supervising a tummy time session for the twins. "Hi, Austin. Hi, Brody. Welcome to our home." Her smile is reassuring, and I relax the tiniest bit knowing I have one ally. Austin steps up next to me and puts his hand on the small of my back. I look up at him and smile. Make that two.

"Thanks so much for having me." I look in both of their directions, but Cole seems determined not to meet my eye, so I decide to focus on the Thomas who doesn't want to murder me. "I brought a little something for you."

"Oh, thank you. You didn't have to bring us anything," Blaire says, taking the wine and flowers I offer. Cole makes a noise, clearly intended to say, "Didn't he?", which Blaire ignores. "Austin's here for dinner at least once a week when it's not festival season, and it's no trouble to set one more place."

She looks down as one of the twins makes a cooing noise. "And this is Cassidy and Melody." I sit myself on the ground next to their blanket, returning the toothless grin Melody gives me. Babies this young are hit or miss whether they scream bloody murder or look up at me in wonder when they come to see me as Santa. It's nice to spend some time in a context with less pressure.

"I have something for you ladies too." I pull out the Santa and Elf teething toys I found at the store last night. "We boiled them in water last night. Is it okay if I hand them over?"

"Oh, Brody, that's so thoughtful. I know they'll love them. The theme choice is very approved in this household." She gives me a wink. A quick glance at Cole shows an impressed look on his face until he realizes I've caught him, and he replaces it with a scowl. I put the toys between the girls. Melody immediately goes for the elf, while Cassidy is more content to show off how she can roll to her back, and reach for the rings above her head. We all sit in silence for a few minutes, watching them being adorable.

Cole clears his throat. "Can I get anyone a drink? We could open the wine you brought?"

"I could have a beer," Austin says.

"Soda water for me," Blaire chimes in.

"I'm good with beer or wine, if you'd like to open it," I say. "In fact, why don't I come help you?" Figure it'll be good to get this out of the way. Then maybe we can all enjoy dinner.

A glimmer of respect flickers in his eyes. "Yeah, why don't you."

Austin plops next to me on the floor before I stand up and squeezes my hand. Blaire gives me a reassuring smile. I take a deep breath and head after Cole into the kitchen.

"Glasses are over there." Cole points with the electric corkscrew he grabbed off the counter. I grab two stemless wine glasses and a highball glass for Blaire. Glasses in hand, I walk to where Cole is peeling off the wine wrapper.

"So," he says.

"So," I repeat, deciding I'll wait and let him say his piece.

"You know I know what happened ten years ago and what's happened since you've been back," he says, his focus fixed on uncorking the wine. I don't think Austin has told him the details of our conversation from Friday night, but I'm not ashamed of it if he has. "You know, why you left the way you did and all. Seems a little selfish to me."

I nod. "At the time, I thought it was selfless, but reflection and therapy have shown me you're right. It only stood to benefit me and what I wanted."

He lifts his head, surprise in his eyes. "Oh."

"Look, I get where you're coming from. Austin means a lot to you. But if you're expecting me to have some ego where I can't admit I was wrong, so you can stay mad, you're not going to find it. I took this job and came here hoping to have a chance to give us both closure. Thinking he'd let me back in, give me more? It was the stuff of dreams. I won't waste it."

He pours us each a glass of wine, the dark red color a contrast to the light countertop. "So what happens after Christmas?" Cole takes several sips of his drink before topping his glass off. I lift my wine to my lips for a single sip, considering my words.

"Again, Cole, I respect the important role you have in Austin's life. He's lucky to have a friend like you—I've never had that, and I can tell you how special it is to see. But right now, we're taking it day by day. When I have a conversation about what's next for the first time, it needs to be with him."

He looks taken aback by my bluntness.

"Know I care about him a lot. I hate the hurt I caused us both ten years ago, and I'm being nothing but honest with him about my feelings now. I can't promise it won't end with us hurt again, but if we do, it won't be because I didn't care enough."

Another sip of wine, and then he speaks. "I can't say that's not fair. Just . . . if Austin wants to go with you this time, hear him out. He's not the same person he was ten years ago either."

A knock on the entryway to the kitchen draws our attention. "We've got about thirty more minutes before the girls start fussing. Are we ready to eat?" Blaire searches between us, satisfied there are no external wounds, at least. "Is that for my soda water?" Her gaze lands on the empty glass.

"Uh, yeah. We got a bit distracted." Cole grabs the other glass and fills it with ice and pours the drink. "I'll get the lasagna out of the oven now."

Blaire takes a sip of the water, offering me a wink, sitting at the table set with festive placemats and Christmas dishes.

We maintain a steady conversation during dinner and through Austin and Cole doing the dishes while Blaire and I sit with the twins. Eventually, it's time for the twins to get their baths and go to sleep upstairs, for however many hours in a row they'll give their parents. Blaire gives us both a hug and heads up the stairs, a twin in each arm.

We're putting on our boots and coats when Cole comes to the door with a bag in his hand. "Here, take the leftover tiramisu with you. We're drowning in Christmas cookies and other treats this time of year from locals grateful for the work on the festival. We won't miss it."

He extends his arm toward me and I take the offering. "Thanks, Cole. Everything was delicious, thanks for cooking and inviting me." Our eyes lock, and I see him give me the smallest of nods. It may not be approval, but it looks a lot like acceptance, and I'll take it.

Cole wraps Austin in a hug, and I wave goodbye as we head out the door.

"Hey, Brody," Cole calls, and I turn from where I stand next to the Bronco. He's standing on the porch, hands shoved in his pockets, probably shivering.

"Yeah?"

"Same time next week?"

I smile. Maybe it's a bit of approval after all.

"Am I invited too?" Austin snarks from the driver's side.

"We'll be here," I respond, before climbing in the car, ready for Austin to take us home.

Chapter 19

Austin

I've worked on some long, grueling jobs over the years. Being an elf in Santa's Workshop six days a week brings with it a next level of exhaustion, along with a new type of satisfaction for the work we're doing. A lot of that is thanks to Brody. The way his enthusiasm is infectious and how many people he's allowing us to help.

But at the same time, the demands playing Santa and his elf isn't super convenient when you have a limited time with the one who got away. I told Brody he never had to go back to the guest room if he didn't want to—and so far, he hasn't. Don't get me wrong, falling into bed together and cuddling all night long is wonderful. So is waking up gradually with lazy handjobs that turn frenzied, or slow, wet blow jobs that rock my world. But I would like to spend time building him up, and then sending him spiraling into the best orgasm of his life.

Brody yawns behind the false wall during our quick evening break, the sounds of *Elf* playing in the background to keep the kids entertained while they wait.

"None of that," I say, and he rolls his eyes at me, a smile on his face. I take a step closer, getting into his space.

Brody swallows as he looks up into my eyes, his darkening as he reads what's on my face. He waits for me to keep talking.

"I have plans for us tonight. And they don't involve you being tired." I whisper the last words in his ear, pretty much beyond caring if the rest of the staff find out Santa and his elf are sleeping together. Blaire knows, and it's a temporary gig. Plus, Jimmy's the one coordinating with Brody's staff back in New York about money things, keeping things clear from any corruption claims.

"Care to tell me about these plans?" He pulls his head back so he can meet my gaze again. "Do you perhaps have a list? Can I check it twice?"

I shake my head. "Nah, I'd rather you use your imagination." I step away to grab some water from the mini fridge, giving Brody some time to daydream, and then banish those thoughts far, far away for the next couple of hours.

Luckily, everyone's anxious for their day off, so cleanup is quick and we're back on the road to Winterberry Glen earlier than normal. I try to make our drive back follow the same theme, but as soon as we pull off school grounds, Brody starts a pattern of tracing his hand from my knee, up my leg before rubbing his thumb over the head of my dick in my jeans, and then taking the return trail back to my knee. With each pass, he spends more time caressing my crotch, and then slows his transition to my knee and back.

The light at the intersection to turn on my street is red, and I strain my hips to push into his hand when it makes contact with my cock again. I groan, restrained by my seat belt when I try to chase his hand as he removes it back to his lap.

"Tell me, is this part of your plan?" he asks, his face innocent, but his gaze wicked.

"You giving me a case of blue balls responsible for removing some of the brain cells responsible for operating a motor vehicle? Yes, right on schedule," I snark, pulling into a parking spot. I throw the SUV in park, undo my seat belt, and lean over the console. My fingers tangle in his hair as I yank his face to mine, devouring his mouth in a kiss I've been aching to give him all day. His tongue tangles with mine, and I swallow down his groan before pulling away.

"We should head inside," I say, taking all my willpower to press pause. "Because the next stage of my plan is much better executed on a bed, and I know you may want to take a shower." I open the door and climb out, surprised to find Brody still in the passenger seat by the time I reach the other side. He's staring into the distance and worrying his lip.

I pull on his door handle and lean down. "Brody? Everything okay?"

He nods. "There's, um, a reason I haven't really pushed to progress things to this point over the past week."

"Oh. Okay," I say, my mind racing with the possibilities. "Do you want to talk about it?"

He nods. "Yeah, I guess we should. Sorry, I killed the mood."

"You didn't kill anything." I wrap my fingers in his and walk with him to the door. "I'm fine if sex isn't penetrative. It's been a long time; tastes change."

Brody smiles warmly at me, relaxing a fraction. "Let's get inside and talk before we scandalize Mrs. Roberts," referring to my next-door neighbor.

I unlock the door, letting us in. "Mrs. Roberts and I share a wall. Unfortunately, I think that ship has sailed."

"*That* definitely doesn't help the mood," he says, and I wince. Yeah, right, talking about my neighbor hearing me have sex with other people is not going to help this situation.

We get unbundled and sit on the couch. Brody plays with a loose thread on the cuff of his sweater. His lip is back between his teeth, which pulls me in two directions: wanting to be the one to bite his lip and wondering what he's going to say. I reach for his cheek, allowing the hairs on his beard to tickle my thumb as I move it up and down, trying to provide some comfort. It must help, because he releases his lip and leans into my hand.

"What's going on?"

Brody swallows and pulls my hand down into his lap, tangling his fingers with mine. "So, I haven't bottomed since we were together."

I hesitate before saying, "Oh, okay," then fall silent while I process.

He winces and tries to pull his hands away, but I tighten my grip. My brain comes back online. "No, I'm sorry, I was processing. You said you were a bottom before, so I'm a little surprised, that's all. What changed? You don't have to have a reason, like I said—preferences shift. It's okay."

His eyes meet mine then, and lock on, where I feel like I couldn't look away even if I wanted to. "I know I'm the one who left, I'm the one who decided, but I need you to know leaving you still wrecked me. It was like I left a part of me behind, and I built a wall around that missing part with law school and busyness, hiding the pain until I could pretend it didn't exist. But that wall also kept people out, stopped them from getting too close to me, from letting them in. It manifested itself physically too—it felt too raw, too vulnerable to let someone into my body that way. Topping meant I could get a physical release without letting my emotions get too involved." His eyes water, but no tears spill over.

I squeeze his hand then, letting him know I hear him, I see him. "I understand not wanting to let anyone get too close. Mine didn't manifest in the same way, but I haven't let anyone in emotionally since you left either."

Brody sniffs and laughs, it sounding a little wet. "Now, I think we've sufficiently killed the mood."

"I mean, if you want to declare the mood dead on arrival, we can. But I think we can resurrect it if we try. I'll go get in the shower and get cleaned up—you go take a minute to breathe and relax on the bed, and we'll see how you feel." I pull Brody to his feet.

"Austin, we don't have to—"

"No, I want to. It's been a while, but it's not like I've never done it before. You'll just need to go slow." The words I say are a stark contrast to the way my emotions are racing ahead, pulling me back into love with this man, and all that he is. "Try not to hurt me." I'll have to keep those emotions locked away—I don't want to make him feel guilty for leaving me twice.

"I haven't done as good a job of it as I should have in the past, but I never want to hurt you ever again."

I lean in to give him a peck on the lips and walk off to the bathroom.

Once I'm clean everywhere I want to be fresh, I wrap a towel around my waist and walk back to my bedroom. I'm wondering if going the towel route is a bit aggressive, considering I'm not sure I'll find Brody too emotionally raw, but the sight on my bed stops me in the doorway.

Brody lies on my bed without a stitch of clothing on. His head and shoulders are propped on a pillow. I spend a few seconds taking in his handsome face, the way the beard that lends so well to his Santa persona now gives him a rugged air I'm very into. The same feelings continue as I take in the way he's let his chest hair grow in, a smattering of grey mixed with the darker brown. The trail of hair narrows as it rises and falls with the curve of his stomach, leading to where his hand is slowly stroking his cock. His legs are splayed on top of the dark blue quilt, and any concerns I had about coming on too strong are long gone. Fuck, he's a pornographic scene laid out to fulfill my fantasies.

"God, baby, you look so good." I watch the heat in his eyes spike at the pet name. I stalk slowly closer to the bed, torn between not wanting to interrupt the show and feeling like I might die if I don't touch him in the next five seconds.

"You look a little overdressed," he says, reaching out and yanking on the towel around my waist until it comes untucked and falls at my feet. I take advantage of the full range of motion to climb onto the bed and straddle his waist, lining my cock up with his. He takes the hint, and widens his fist, wrapping around both of us as best he can, adding a small thrust of his hips to the motion. Our cocks glide together, and I spot the bottle of lube next to him on the bed.

"God, you're smart," I say, leaning down to kiss him. I thrust my hips into his fist in time with his and moan into his mouth.

"It pays to check things twice," he murmurs against my mouth before slipping his tongue in to tangle with mine. He releases our cocks and moves his hands to my hips. His fingers dig into my ass cheeks as his grip tightens, increasing the pressure as we continue to thrust into each other.

"I could come like this and die happy," he says. "But you did get yourself squeaky clean for me, and I would really love to fuck you." His hips circle at "fuck you" while he speaks against my mouth, and I have to break his hold so my dick is dangling in the air, touching nothing else. Hearing his desire for me, mixed with the smooth slide of his cock against mine almost ended this party too soon.

I look down at his swollen lips and shining eyes, cheeks flushed red from pleasure. "Your move, Santa."

Chapter 20

Brody

I don't know that I've ever slept with a guy who knows I'm a professional Santa. Getting hit on as Santa isn't novel to me, but mixing together all the parts of me is. I've never wanted someone to know all of me the same way I want Austin to.

I wrap my leg around his and flip him so I'm on top. His eyes darken.

"I don't get to be thrown around a lot. I'm into it."

A growl comes from deep in my throat as I lean down to attack his mouth. "I throw you around. Only me." I'm not normally a possessive guy, but something in Austin brings it out in me.

"Yes, sir," he says breathlessly as he recovers from the assault of my lips. My mind is on keeping him breathless as I trail kisses from his mouth, down his neck. I nip at his collarbone, before moving across his chest to the other side. Austin's hips arch up, searching for friction with my body. I'm keeping my cock out of range intentionally, and he whines when he doesn't find the contact he's looking for.

"Patience," I murmur into his skin before biting one of his nipples. I lick the sting away. My cock is leaking all over, but that's not important now. What's important is lying underneath me, grinding himself against the trail of hair on my stomach. I love that I get to see him like this. I take even that limited contact away as I continue my path downward, licking the grooves of his abs as he clenches against the sensation of my tongue. Instead of continuing straight down to take his cock in my mouth, I lick the crease of his thighs, breathing in the smell of his soap and pure Austin. Delaying where we both want my mouth to be, I take one ball in my mouth, and then the other. Not able to wait any longer to feel the weight of him on my tongue, I finally give in, licking a stripe from his base to his tip before circling the head of his cock.

While my mouth is busy, I bring a finger and push gently on his hole. Even with the attention on his dick, I feel his muscles clench at the smallest of intrusions. I trust Austin to be honest with me about what he wants, but I know it's been a long time, he may need some extra attention. Luckily, giving Austin attention has once again become one of my favorite pastimes.

I pull my mouth off his cock, and admire how it glistens with his pre-cum and my saliva against his abs. His eyes meet mine, and I keep my motions slow and deliberate. With a hand around the back of each thigh, I push his legs up and open, baring all of him to me.

"Hello there," I say, taking in how his puckered hole is waiting for my attention. He wraps his hands behind his thighs, helping me to keep them up. "I'd like to eat your ass to start," I say, gently brushing my fingers across his hole, to his balls, before giving his cock a gentle stroke, noticing it starting to soften with all the attention and exposure.

Austin's eyes widen, and he nods.

"Use your words, please," I say, my tone stern. I know we've never done this, I'm not sure if anyone else has had him this way either. Pleasure zings through me at knowing I might be the only one.

"Yes," he breathes, his eyes showing his nervous anticipation.

"Would you like to lay like this? On your knees might be easier," I offer.

"No, I . . . I want to see your face."

I smile, feeling the same way. "Pass me a pillow please." He does as I ask and helps me prop his hips up, putting it into place. I scoot further down the bed, bringing myself eye level with my goal. I circle his hole with my tongue before brushing over the area in soft and gentle strokes. He moans, "Oh fuck," and I take his enjoyment as a green light to keep going.

I take my time, feeling him relax. The tip of my tongue breaches the ring of muscle, and he tightens, pushing me back out.

"Ugh, sorry. I'm trying to relax," he mutters, adjusting the grip on his legs.

"You won't hear me complain—I could spend hours between your legs." I reach up to give his cock a gentle stroke, combining my touch with more attention to the outer ring. Again, I poke the tip of my tongue inside him, and this time, his body lets me in a bit further. I alternate between quick strokes across his hole and thrusting my tongue deeper inside him. His groans grow louder and more frequent the more he lets me in.

"More, I need more," he says, his fingers scrambling for the bottle of lube I got out while he was in the shower and shoving it toward me.

"Topping from the bottom," I tut, making sure my tone is teasing. Squeezing out a bit of the liquid, I warm it between my fingers before brushing across the puckered skin with one finger. I slowly push it in, pushing past the muscles trying to keep me out. In and out, slowly, until I'm down to the third knuckle. I sit up on my knees, so I can watch his whole body for reactions. My other hand around his cock, I keep my eyes on his face as I aim for—

"Oh, fuck," he shouts, his hips leaving the bed. "Fuck, it's not nearly as good when I do it."

"I'm definitely putting watching you play with your ass on my

Christmas list," I say, thrusting my finger against his prostate again. "Are you ready for another one?" I ask, wanting to check in at every stage.

"Yes, please, two more even." His tone is desperate, sending a jolt of lust straight to my cock.

"One at a time, babe," I say, before dribbling more lube on my hand and pushing a second finger in. I keep my grip loose on his cock, adding a stroke in every once in a while to keep him on his toes. Probably unnecessary with the prostate stimulation, but I'm nothing if not a giver.

"Forget the third one. Fuck me, please," he says, his eyes closed and back straining.

"Uh-uh," I say, scissoring my fingers to open him up even more while I drag my other hand up and down his stomach, lighting up his nerve endings. "We gotta do three first before I give you this fat cock."

His eyes open and land right on my cock before he swallows hard. "Okay, yes, third finger. But make it quick."

I kiss the inside of his knee. "I love how you're begging for my dick, but I won't hurt you. It'll be worth it, I promise." I push a third finger in. After a few thrusts, Austin's meeting my hand with his hips. Maybe he really is ready for me.

I pull my hand out and set Austin's feet on the bed to give his legs a break. "I got tested since the last time I was with someone, but I can use a condom if you want."

Austin reaches for his bedside table and pulls out a foil packet. "I'll go get tested tomorrow. I always wear a condom, but to be safe for now." He hands the condom to me and watches as I roll the silicone down my length and pour lube into my palm. His strokes to his cock match the strokes I use to spread the lube over the silicone, a lazy smile on his face.

Once I'm slick for him, I walk my knees forward a bit and he grabs his legs again without me asking. The head of my cock rests against his opening and our eyes meet.

"Are you ready?" I ask, holding still.

"Ready," he responds. My focus shifts to where he's swallowing me in, bit by bit. "So tight," I murmur, checking to be sure he's doing okay. His eyes are on my face.

"So full," he answers, and a second later, I bottom out, my pelvis meeting his ass. I lean over his body to kiss him, unable to resist while I give him time to adjust.

Rising up a few inches, I find his gaze waiting for mine. I move my hips, pulling out a few inches, before pushing slowly back in. The slow slide repeats until Austin reaches up and tangles his hand in my hair, pulling my mouth back to his. "More," he says, the word almost lost as he tangles his tongue with mine, giving me everything he's got. I start thrusting faster and harder, his hips finding the pace and matching me.

I adjust the angle of my body slightly and know I've found my goal when Austin pulls his mouth from mine. With his head thrown back, he groans long and loud. "Right. There." Happy to oblige, I pick up the pace, slamming into him hard enough the headboard joins into the rhythm of skin meeting skin, our heavy breaths and groans. The soundtrack of my wet dreams.

Austin's arm snakes between us and I feel the knuckles of his hand moving up and down his cock against my stomach. "Almost there," he says, his voice breathless. "Get there too."

All of a sudden, I'm right at the edge, teetering on beating him. I put the last bit I have into those final thrusts and feel his muscles squeeze me like a vice while the rest of his body tightens and he spills onto his stomach. My hips stutter before I'm emptying into the condom. My arms give out, and I feel the warm wetness of his release between us. His legs cross over the back of my calves while his arms tighten across my back. I shift, trying to roll to the side, but he tightens his hold, not letting me. "Feels good. Like my own Brody-scented weighted blanket." He talks into my neck, and I feel the exhale of his laughter as I laugh too.

After a moment, I pull up to look in his eyes, and the contentment I find there spreads through me like the warmth of a bath I would love to sink into every fucking day. I take his lips in a gentle kiss before finding the strength to push myself up slightly. He lets me go this time, and I slowly pull out, not missing the wince he tries to hide. "Let me go get something to clean us up." I dispose of the condom and walk naked to the bathroom. I wet a cloth and leave the faucet running while I wipe the cum from my stomach and chest hair before it dries. Once the water warms, I run the water over it, and walk quickly back to Austin before it cools.

He's in the exact position I left him, with his eyes closed. He blinks as I use the wash cloth where he's a little pink from my intrusion. Once I've tended to him thoroughly there, I wipe up his stomach and chest. "It helps you're not furry like me," I say, passing over his smooth skin. He reaches for me, and I go easily, tossing the cloth onto the floor to be dealt with later. His fingers run through the hair on my chest, trailing over my stomach and making the return path.

"I dunno, I'm a fan of furry Brody. Though I guess you could do this yourself if you wanted."

"It could never feel as good as you touching me," I respond, pressing my forehead to his. "Good?" I ask, referring to more of him than the fingers tracing my body.

"Good," he says nodding, his eyes closing again.

I position us so his head rests in the crook of my neck, an arm around his back, curling him into my body. He comes willingly and tangles his legs with mine, erasing the few inches he has on me. His fingers continue their trail, slowing as his breathing evens out and then stopping right over my heart. Like his body knows, even in his sleep he belongs there, because that organ belongs to him. Sometimes, I think it never stopped. I cover his hand with mine and follow him into sleep.

Chapter 21

Austin

Despite the intense physical activities of last night, I'm awake with the sun this morning. I slide out from under Brody's arm slung across my waist, hoping slow movements will let him sleep. He rolls over, but burrows deeper into his pillow, his breathing still even and deep.

I wince slightly as I get dressed. Brody took good care of me last night, but there's little doubt I'll have reminders of how we spent our evening. No complaints here.

Ten minutes later, I've freshened up in the bathroom and left a note for Brody on the dining room table. The clinic opens at seven, and I need to go visit my mom today. She's up before the birds every morning, so I'll grab some pastries from the coffee shop next door and head over there afterward. That should leave most of the day for whatever Brody has in mind—finally decorating the tree we bought last week and lying horizontal on the couch are my votes.

I'm in and out at the clinic and should have results in under forty-eight hours. The idea of nothing between us as Brody slides into me makes me chub up a bit when I'm in line for our coffees.

All my attention goes to reading the specials board, needing a different train of thought before I get to my mom's.

Two coffees and two bags of pastries later, and I'm off to the house I grew up in on the edge of Winterberry Glen. I try to decide which croissant Brody will like more as I cross through the familiar streets, making it to the other side of our small town in under ten minutes, even hitting a few red lights along the way.

I pull into the driveway behind my mom's CR-V and cut the engine. There are a few cars parked in front of the house along the street. While I walk to the front door, I wonder if she's hosting a Zumba class in her living room again, or if Mrs. Benson across the street has family visiting.

The doorbell rings, and I look around the front of the house while I wait for her to answer. I fixed the steps before the first snow earlier this winter, and they seem to be holding up all right. The light blue siding we replaced a few years back could probably use a good power washing once the weather warms up. I'm straightening the wreath on her front door, wondering what's taking so long, when the door swings inward and the wreath comes off the hook in my hand.

"Austin!" my mom greets me, a little flushed. "I wasn't expecting you this early today. Come in, get out of the cold." I hang the wreath back where it belongs, still a little crooked, and step into the hug my mom has waiting for me.

"Yeah, I woke up early, and thought I'd get a start on the day. Plus, I brought pastries." I hold up the bag and coffee holder in my hands. A noise from the kitchen draws my attention, and I look over to see my mom's three best friends clearing up a stack of papers from the table.

"Oh, hi, ladies. I have enough to share if you're interested? Wanted to be sure we had choices." Doris, who my mom has known since high school, opens her mouth to respond, then looks behind me and shuts it firmly. "No, no, we won't impose. We were just leaving." Betsy and Laurel each squeeze my arm on their way out the door behind Doris, with promises to call my mom later.

"Let's get those pastries on a plate. Does the coffee need to be warmed up?" My mom moves past me into the kitchen and busies herself getting down plates and grabbing silverware.

"No, it should be okay. Malcolm found a biodegradable type of stopper, so he has those out again. What's going on? I have never answered less than two questions each from your friends, even when I was sick on the couch in elementary school or trying to sneak in past curfew in high school."

"Oh, you know, they have Christmas shopping to do. It's a really busy time of year." She avoids my eyes, arranging the baked goods in a ring around the edge of the plate like she's expecting company.

"Okay, you're freaking me out. Did the doctor call back? Did something show up on your tests?"

My mom sits down and grabs my hand. "Oh, honey, no. I'm sorry. Nothing like that at all. I'm feeling great."

"Okay, then why the weird vibes?"

She sighs and then pulls a brochure out of her pocket, handing it to me. "I wanted to wait until you were done with the elf gig to tell you about this. I know how busy you've been, shacking up with your ex-boyfriend and hiding it from me," she teases.

Brochure in my hand forgotten, my jaw drops open. "How do you know about Brody staying with me?"

"Oh please, you know I go to book club at Ridge Reads almost every week. I had to listen to the all the ladies talk about hot Santa and his devoted elf. Plus, you know I never forget a face, even when it's grown a beard and aged very handsomely. When they showed me a picture, I knew it was Brody."

I cover my eyes with the brochure in my hand before meeting her gaze. She's smiling at me, and I'm thankful she's not actually mad. "I wanted to tell you, but I also don't really know how to explain it. He's here, but in a couple of weeks he won't be . . ."

"It's okay, honey." She squeezes my hand. "I know how much you loved him, and you're getting a second chance. It would be hard for almost anyone to resist. Besides, you're not the only one keeping things close to the chest." She nods at the papers in my hand, which she apparently didn't hand to me so I'd have something to hide behind.

I unfold the glossy brochure and take in bright pictures of a living community, with blue skies, palm trees, and a lot of people my mom's age looking happy. The words come into focus and I home in on one.

"Florida?" I ask. She always joked about retiring to Florida, escaping these cold New England winters after I was "grown." But we had to tap into a lot of her savings when she got sick, and she stopped talking about it after a while.

Mom nods. "Florida. This community takes college dorm-style living and sets it up for old biddies like myself. Four single rooms on one level, shared common spaces, and best of all, shared costs."

The strange behavior all makes sense now. "So all four of you are going together."

She nods. "It's our New Year's resolution to be there before the end of next year."

"Well, I'm glad you won't be alone. I know you gals can take care of each other." And I mean it. I learned about loyalty and friendship from these ladies. The way they stepped up when Mom had to work late and were always chatting late into the night over glasses of wine when I should have been sleeping. The way they stepped up and made sure we always had food and the house was always clean while she was sick. "You'll be in good hands." We sit in silence for a moment.

"Well," I say, clearing the emotion from my throat. "If this is your last New England Christmas, we better make it count. But I draw the line at letting you decorate a palm tree—you've gotta take some traditions with you."

"Sounds like a deal." She squeezes my hand once more before

selecting a chocolate croissant from the plate and leaning back in her chair. "So tell me, what's life like as an elf to a professional Santa? And when are you bringing Santa by for dinner?"

"Soon, Mom. I hope very soon."

Epistolary Interlude # 2

AUSTIN

Where are you?

BRODY

I've been gone for twenty minutes.

AUSTIN

It feels like two hours.

BRODY

You're the one who guilted me into making this Peppermint Chocolate dessert for dinner tomorrow night and told me to go to the store when I suggested we just pick up a cake at Jitter's instead

AUSTIN

I may have made a big deal about how good this dessert is going to be to Blaire. We may have money riding on its being better than Cole's tiramisu.

BRODY

No pressure.

AUSTIN

Besides my foot hurts.

BRODY

I offered to go get the car and pick you up so you didn't have to walk back to the gym. That not-so-little boy did land on it really hard.

AUSTIN

You should have carried me, bridal style.

BRODY

I'm more of a piggyback kinda guy.

AUSTIN

Yeah, you are.

BRODY

I'm so afraid to look at Urban Dictionary right now.

AUSTIN

Well, hurry up. Safely.

Because the clinic just posted my test results, all negative, and I have gotten into the drawer to celebrate. 😌🍆

BRODY

Did you reach for something blue and long?

AUSTIN

Maybe . . .

BRODY

Damnit, I told you I wanted to watch.

AUSTIN

Guess you better hurry then.

BRODY

Don't let yourself come. I'll be there in fifteen.

AUSTIN

Ohh, topping from the top. Yes, sir.

From: admin@walkersantaco.com
To: brody@walkersantaco.com
December 16
Re: Hudson Associates Christmas Party

Dear Mr. Walker,
As we've discussed over the past few weeks, I'm still concerned about
the assignment of Ted to the Hudson Associates Christmas Party.
We've received another complaint about his behavior at a function
last evening. I think you may need to speak with him, and soon.

Please let me know if there's any other action you'd like from me
on this matter.

Warmest Regards,
Monica

COLE

Now that I've gotten over the betrayal of my
wife liking another man's desserts more than
mine . . . Can you ask Brody if I can have the
recipe?

BLAIRE

Would you rather I lied to you?

COLE

Sometimes, a little white lie doesn't hurt.

AUSTIN

He says he'll email it to you right now. And he said if the tiramisu recipe isn't a family secret, he'd love to try his hand at making it one day.

COLE

What do you think, Austin? Is he one to be trusted with family recipes? I feel like maybe someday I'll be letting him in on the family secret ingredient.

AUSTIN

Blaire, I can tell you the secret ingredient I added to the dessert for tonight.

COLE

Nope, don't want to know.

AUSTIN

What?! I just put a little extra pep in his step, so he could sprinkle it with love.

COLE

I really hope you don't mean love as a euphemism for something else.

BLAIRE

What are you, twelve? Of course not. So, love, huh?

AUSTIN

Oh, whoops, there's a weird cell phone outage that's only affecting my apartment. Your messages can't be delivered, don't call here again.

Love you both. Night.

MOM

Thank you both for coming over for dinner on your day off.

AUSTIN

Is this a group chat? How did you get Brody's number?

BRODY

It was great to see you again, Mrs. Owens. Thank you for cooking. 😊

MOM

You're a charmer. Yes, the finest plating of food out of a metal containers this side of the Pine River.

AUSTIN

Hello? Am I invisible? How is this happening?

MOM

Brody gave me his number so I could forward him the information about the solstice celebration on Friday.

AUSTIN

Oh my God, Mom. Seriously?

BRODY

I thought it could enhance my role as Santa to brush up on other winter holidays and celebrations.

AUSTIN

We have to turn around and go to work the next morning.

BRODY

I thought we could see how we feel and maybe make an appearance.

MOM

I'll put you both down as a maybe.

BRODY

That's very kind of you, Mrs. Owens. I hope we can make it.

MOM

Please call me Brenda.

AUSTIN

What is happening right now?

To: brody@walkersantaco.com
From: mwalker@walkerfoundation.org
CC: admin@walkerfoundation.org
December 19
Re: Holiday Plans

Dear Brody,
I'm so sorry I've missed our last few catch-up calls. This time of year is so busy with service events and other commitments. I can't wait to see you before too long.

Have you solidified your holiday plans for next week yet? I imagine you may spend Christmas Day with your beau in Winterberry Glen, but wasn't sure when you'd be heading back this way. If you'll be in town for New Year's, I'd love to make a reservation for us for dinner. Should I make it for three? Let me and Sally, copied here, know.

Love,
Grandma

Hi, Blaire, Austin gave me your number. I hope that's okay.

Of course! You probably had it already, it's listed in your onboarding email.

Right. Well, it's better this way, because this is a personal matter, not business.

Oh, do tell.

I feel as if you're the type of person one could be in cahoots with about a Christmas present surprise.

Literally my favorite type of cahoots. Tell me everything.

It'll be easier to explain in person. Can we meet for coffee before the workshop opens tomorrow? Say 10:30?

Yes. Hmm . . . how to get Austin to bring you over early . . .

BRODY

> I'm going to try to sneak out early and take a rideshare, but a backup plan is a good one.

BLAIRE

> Just make sure to wear him out good tonight.

> Sorry, that's inappropriate. I had another half glass of wine after I finished my first.

> You could also tell him I want to talk to you about a contract for next year's festival. Because I do. See, business and pleasure.

> Please forget I said pleasure.

BRODY

> I'm blushing, but I feel like the cahoots has already started. See you tomorrow.

To: aowens@gmail.com
From: tourism@winterberryglen.gov
December 20
Re: Setting up meeting for first week of January

Hi Austin,

Richard Harris here with the Winterberry Glen tourism office. Well, a one-man office. But that's what I'd like to schedule a time to talk to you about after the first of the year. Can you please get back to me with your availability at your earliest convenience? This is my last day in the office for the year, but I'll be checking emails regularly.

Looking forward to connecting.

Best,
Richard

Chapter 22

Brody

The last family of the final weekend day of this holiday season walks out the door, the kids waving all the way. The air is jubilant. We saw more people in the last two days than we have any other weekend this month without any major hiccups. One more full day tomorrow and special hours on Christmas Eve the next day, and another Santa season will be behind us. It's always the same—looking back, I can't believe how fast it's flown by. It seems to be faster every year.

Austin laughs at something Jimmy is saying over by the donation station. I know I'm smiling like a fool while I watch him. Maybe there's good reason this season has felt so light. It's been easy to forget my time here is temporary and that Austin and I still haven't talked about what happens when I have to go back to Stamford.

The season has been such a success not only because I have Austin back in my life, but the crew here is one of the best I've ever worked with. I need to make sure it gets on Monica's list for January to offer Jimmy a consulting contract to figure out how to implement his system throughout all the long-term gigs we do next year. It may be the perfect thing to help us level up.

Jimmy and Austin are still engrossed when I stand up to stretch. Walking around to the other side of the false wall behind my chair, I fish my phone out of my pocket. Monica's name pops up when I wake the device up, like she knew I was thinking about her. The call ends before I can get to it, and I see I have another fifteen missed calls from her over the last two hours since our last break.

"Shit," I mutter, hitting call.

"Oh, Brody, thank God. I mean, Mr. Walker, hello." She sounds more flustered than I've heard her in the three years since I hired her, and she's held this company together by seven threads all pulling in different directions more than once.

"Brody is fine, Monica. What's going on?"

"It's Ted."

"Fuck," I say. I tried to get in touch with Ted a couple of times since I got Monica's email last week, but he never returned any of my calls or emails. I had hoped his silence meant he got himself together.

"Fuck, indeed. He got arrested."

"On a—"

"He wasn't on a job. He was off today since he's scheduled for the Hudson party tomorrow."

"What happened?" I say, rubbing my hand over my face. Ted going off the rails like this doesn't make sense. He's been one of our most reliable employees since we hired him two years ago. It's why I cut him so much slack all season, despite Monica's concern.

"His wife called me after she heard from the station. She shared with me he's facing some scary health news, and it's caused him to relapse after eight years sober. He got picked up for drunk and disorderly."

"Oh god, how awful," I say. "Did you get a contact number for her to call her back? I'd love to call her personally next week, offer help in whatever way we can."

"It's already in your inbox with a list of highly recommended rehab facilities in the area. I had to do something while you weren't answering your phone because you're so committed to your job."

"Next research project is to figure out where you want to go on vacation in February, on me."

"Let's make it through this week, and then we can talk about how you'll make it up to me," she says. "There's no one available to cover the job tomorrow. Even the temps we hired to fill in are all assigned. Your reliability and success are going to be your downfall."

I chew on my lip. "We have to have someone there, and it can't be just anyone either. Hudson Associates' donation is the largest from a single group we receive every year."

"I think we're going to have to pull out of the last contract we signed. Especially because it comes with the escape clause with you as the owner fulfilling it. I'm making myself a note to ask legal if we can actually change the language to that, because when I'm not so stressed, it's going to be hilarious."

As soon as Monica told me Ted got arrested, I knew in the back of my mind this was the solution. It's my company, the charity arm is my passion project. This has to fall at my feet.

"You're right . . . I'll figure something out here. I guess I need to look at a train schedule. Or would a plane be better? I'd have to figure out how to get to the airport in Boston, but . . ."

"Brody." Monica snaps me out of it, her tone indicating what she thinks of me acting like she doesn't have this sorted. "The trains are sold out tomorrow, and there's a storm predicted to hit in the morning with winds starting tonight. The last train leaves from Springfield in two hours. You need to be on it."

"Understood," I say, my stomach sinking into my shoes. I may not be disappearing in the middle of the night this time, but I am leaving unexpectedly and need to ask the man I'm saying goodbye to to take me to the train station. All of a sudden, our shared reluctance to talk about the future, about what this means and how we can make it work, seems ridiculous. "Can you send me a

—" My phone vibrates in my hand, and I know exactly what I'll find when I look. "Ticket?" I finish unnecessarily.

"I've booked you into Penn Station and will call the dry cleaners down the street from your grandma's telling them to expect your suit first thing in the morning. Do you want me to call her to let her know you're coming?"

"No, I'll call her from the train and let her know. Thank you for everything, Monica, honestly. I'll see you in the morning?"

"You're buying coffee, for sure." And with that, she's gone.

"Train? Morning?" Austin's voice comes from behind me, and I close my eyes, wishing I could be anywhere else right now. But I know I have to face this. I have to tell him what's happening.

I turn around and see Austin there, elf hat in hand, looking crestfallen. Whatever he reads on my face causes his expression to harden.

"Something's cropped up at work—an emergency with one of my Santas, and I need to go back to the city to cover for him. The company that's hosting its Christmas party tomorrow night is the largest single donor we have. I can't lose out on their donation, for the people who work for me, and the people the money goes to help."

Austin's face softens, his eyes turning understanding. "When do you leave?"

I look at my phone and swear. "The train leaves in less than two hours, and it's over an hour from here, longer from Winter-berry Glen."

"Well, we better get a move on then. Tiffany, can you cover cleanup for us?" Austin asks a passing elf, who nods, winking at us as we exit and walk quickly back to the gym to change. If only we were sneaking out early for something sexy, and not to embark on what might be the longest, yet still entirely too short, car ride of my life.

We get into Austin's SUV, and he plugs the train station into the GPS. "There's a little bit of traffic, but it looks like we will get there about twenty minutes before the train leaves. I don't think we have enough time to go back to my place to get anything."

I try to hide my wince at him calling it his place again. "I think you're right, especially if traffic backs up any further. My assistant said the trains tomorrow are sold out, and there's a good chance flights will get canceled tomorrow with an incoming storm. I can't miss it."

"You'll be okay without your meds?" he asks, even while turning out of the high school away from Winterberry Glen and toward the highway.

I nod. "I can get an emergency prescription for my migraine meds." And I don't want to need PrEP ever again, I think to myself, but don't say it out loud. I need to say something about what's next for us, but I have no idea where to start.

"You should call Blaire," Austin says. "I'm sure we can find someone, somewhere, who can fill in as Santa for a day and a half. They may not be a professional, but it's the end of the festival, and we don't want to let all the kids down." And if there was any part of me that wasn't in love with him before, it just tumbled over the line into heads over heels.

I pull out my phone, hovering over Blaire's number, when it hits me.

"You should do it. You should be Santa."

Chapter 23

Austin

If I wasn't so focused on keeping my eyes on the road to avoid looking at Brody before, his words may have killed us.

"I'm sorry, what?"

"You'll need to find a beard and some theater glue, but I have to imagine in a town like Holly Ridge, someone has one in their closet."

I laugh, assuming he must be kidding. "I can't be Santa. I'm sarcastic and unreliable. A flight risk. That's not jolly and reliable old Saint Nick.

"Austin," Brody says. Something in his tone makes me take my eyes off the road to glance at his face. The serious and earnest expression is illuminated by a passing light near a highway exit. "You're none of those terrible things you just said about yourself. Well, you are sarcastic, but it's all part of your charm, and I'm positive you can rein it in for twelve hours over two days."

"Still, I—"

"Your first thought when driving your live-in ex-boyfriend, turned fuck-buddy, turned whatever-we're-not-saying to the train station with no notice is to not disappoint the kids of this community, to make sure your friend has a heads-up. I'm not sure it gets much more Santa than that. You've been standing next to me for weeks. I know you can do it. You can wear one of my suits."

I mull over his words, his unwavering faith and belief in me overwhelming my senses. "Okay. You're sure I can wear one of your suits?"

"Absolutely. There's no one else I would trust to take care of them like I do." His voice is full of emotion, but like he said, we're still not talking about it. We've always had a ticking clock over us. Maybe we were able to snooze it or brush the countdown away before now. It felt nebulous. The workshop closes up on the twenty-fourth, but who wants to travel on Christmas? I knew he had to go back to Stamford, to New York eventually, but it wasn't set in stone. Now, the clock has been wound forward, it's blinking in bright red and sounding the alarm. Suddenly, we're down to minutes rather than days.

"I'll have to come back to get my stuff, you know. Or maybe you could bring it down in a few days?"

"Well, with it being my mom's last Christmas in Winterberry Glen, at least in her house, I think I want to stay around here. But you could come back and join us for sure. The Gingerbread Ball for New Year's is a little corny, but a good time. I'm sure you'd be a guest of honor."

I see Brody's head nod out of the corner of my eye. My hands tighten around the steering wheel as I keep looking ahead, afraid the roadblocks springing up between us may manifest themselves on the actual road ahead.

"Right, of course. It would be great to see everyone from town while not wearing a red velvet suit. It's very possible Grams is going to guilt me into staying in the city with her for the rest of the week."

It's hard to swallow past the lump growing in my throat. "Sure, I know you guys are close, and you being here for so long was a surprise." It's the guy's grandma—how can I fault him for wanting to spend time with her? "And then I know January is busy for you all, wrapping up the season and getting tax stuff done."

He clears his throat. Maybe I'm not the only one experiencing a lump. "Yeah, but then the administrative staff tends to take most of February off. I often travel somewhere. Maybe you could come with me?"

Images of Brody and me on a tropical beach, sharing an over-sized lounger, sipping cocktails, flashes in my mind for a second before I force them away. "I have that meeting with the guy from the tourism office the first week of January. Depending on what his offer is and if I take it, I probably can't ask for time off right away."

"Right, of course not. I think it'll be really great for you. I can't wait to hear what he has to say." The silence stretches between us. I'm positive Brody will be the first person I want to tell about how the meeting goes. But right now, I don't feel sure he'll pick up the phone if I call—or if I'll be able to bring myself to risk only getting his voicemail.

Luckily, you have a best friend who will be excited to be the first to hear your news. And then he'll go tell his wife, and they'll hold their babies and be a perfect family, while you go home. Alone. Where there's no one waiting with a warm cooked meal or convincing you to buy an inflatable you don't need. Maybe that's how it's supposed to be—the plus one in everyone else's story.

I shake myself and focus my attention on the mileposts as they tick by. No other thoughts except the numbers, bringing me closer to losing Brody—again.

It's silent until I turn on the signal for the exit to take us to the train station.

"We can figure this out, you know. I really believe we can," Brody says, desperation in his voice.

The clicking of the turn signal fills the car again as I pull into the train station, so conveniently located right off the highway. The predicted traffic on the GPS never materialized, and we're here thirty minutes before departure, like Amtrak suggests for this station.

I turn the car off, and the silence deepens without the sound of the engine, the whir of the tires.

"Even if we can't," I say, my words slow and measured, "I'm glad we had this Christmas miracle." My voice catches on the word Christmas, and I feel a tear spill from my eye. Brody's hand reaches out. His touch is gentle as he turns my head to face him. His eyes glisten, and I see a tear track down his cheek, disappearing into his beard.

"I'll never forget it, like I never forgot you." His grip tightens as he pulls me to him, and our lips meet, salty with tears, tasting of hanging onto the last shreds of hope and something a lot like love.

"I don't want to say goodbye," he whispers when he pulls back, tipping his forehead to mine.

"Then we won't," I whisper back. We stay still for a moment more before he presses a gentle kiss to my lips. He pulls back, reaching into the back seat for his garment bag, and climbs out of the car. Two taps on the door after he shuts it serve as his departing notice, and I watch as he walks to the station. I feel like I could burst. It can't end like this.

Unbuckling, I lean halfway out the window. "Hey, Brody!" He turns and looks at me. "Merry Christmas."

Thanks to a well-placed streetlight, I can see him smile. "Merry Christmas, Austin."

I stay where I am as he turns back around and continues his path, until he's through the door and out of sight. Only then do I sit myself back in the driver's seat and turn the car on. The radio turns on automatically, and Christmas music fills the small space. I push the button to silence the cheer, and head back to the highway, with only my thoughts for company.

❄

Back in Winterberry Glen, I can't bring myself to go back to my apartment, knowing there will be pieces of Brody everywhere. I know I can't avoid it forever, but I can at least for tonight. Instead, I pull into my mom's driveway. After I turn the car off, I sit still for a moment, exhausted. How in the world am I supposed to put on that suit tomorrow and be what those kids need? All I want is to sleep for a week.

The front door opens, and I see my mom's silhouette back lit through the storm door. If I don't get out to explain why I'm here, she'll knock on my car window in a few minutes. Once I step onto the front porch, she looks at me questioningly. "He's gone, Mom," is all I can manage. She opens the door wider, ushering me in. "Let's make some hot chocolate."

A few minutes later we're sitting on the couch, steaming mugs of cocoa in hand. The only lights in the living room are the ones on the Christmas tree in the corner, and music is softly playing from the stereo.

"So what happened?" she asks. "You were getting along like gangbusters the other night."

I take a sip of chocolate to fortify me and prepare to explain. "He got a call from his assistant. Something happened with one of his Santas and an important gig. He had to go back to New York tonight or risk getting stuck in a storm and not making it tomorrow."

"Well, how did he get to the train station?"

"I mean, I took him. I understand why he had to leave. It just hurts he's not coming back."

She puts her mug down on the coffee table and turns fully toward me. A sign she means business. "He said so, point blank?"

"I mean, not exactly. We talked about different times we could see each other, but there are some roadblocks in the way. And anyway, after he gets back to the city and leaves the bubble of Winterberry Glen and us living together, he's not going to want me any—"

"Austin Michael Owens." Even at thirty-six, getting full-named has me sitting up straighter. "Why do you find it so hard to believe you're easy to love?" I open my mouth to reply, but she holds up her hand. "That boy loves you. I see it in the way he looks at you, cares for you, accepts texts from your mother about celebrations he surely had no interest in going to hours before. I see it in the way, after all these years, he came back for you. Why wouldn't he make the effort to see you after work called him away?"

I shrug. "His life is there, and my life is here."

"And does it always have to be that way?"

"Well, no, I guess not. But you're here, and then there's the possibility of a job with the tourism board . . ."

"Sweetie, I love you. But a maybe job at the tourism board? You'd be bored senseless in a minute. I'm so blessed to have brought you into this world, to have had all this time together, good and bad, living so close. Besides, soon I won't be living here anymore, so you can take that out of the equation."

"I mean, a job that contributes to my health insurance would be nice," I mumble, mostly because I need to defend myself a little bit.

"I think they have those in New York, or in Stamford too, you know."

"But what about Christmas? The last one in this house?"

"A house is a house. It's the people who make it a home. It's time you put finding your home first. Besides, you know I won't be alone. People are always wandering in and out—it's a Christmas open house."

I'm quiet for a moment, thinking back to my conversation with Brody in the car on the way to the train station. He tried so many times to tell me he didn't want this to be over, but I couldn't meet him in the middle. Instead, I shut him down, deflecting out of fear I'm not worth the effort. I'm going to need to go the whole way to him this time. It's only fair. After all, he came the whole way to me.

"That's the face of a man who's developing a plan," Mom says, picking her hot chocolate back up and taking a satisfied sip.

"One's definitely starting to take shape. I promised Brody I'd fill in as Santa tomorrow and Tuesday, but I can drive to him in the afternoon. The storm should have passed by then. If you're really sure it's okay I'm not here on Christmas."

"Seeing my son happy after all he's done for me is the only Christmas present I need. Now get out of here, I paused a new Hallmark movie when you showed up at my door all mopey." She softens her words with a smile, knowing full well she would have talked it through all night if I needed her to. I lean forward and kiss her on the cheek before taking quick steps to the door.

"Dinner tomorrow night?" I say over my shoulder when I reach the front door.

"It's a date. Now get out!" The sounds of a city gal and small town guy falling in love fill the living room, and I smirk. Gender identity aside, sometimes life is just like the movies.

Back in the Bronco, I dial Blaire's number.

"Blaire, I'm going to ask you to be unethical for me. But if things go like I think they might, you'll have a guaranteed Holly Ridge Santa for a long, long time."

Chapter 24

Brody

Even fresh out of the shower, I'm still shaking away the fog of a late afternoon nap. I haven't slept well since I got back to New York. The party last night was a success, and Mr. Hudson Senior himself told me their largest donation yet would be arriving next week. I joined in with the Santas visiting the children's hospital this morning, hoping that keeping myself busy would allow me to forget, for at least a couple minutes at a time, how miserable I am. It almost worked, bringing joy to those kids who don't get to be at home on Christmas. But an aching feeling in my gut lingered in the background.

I felt a migraine coming on after I got home, so even though it likely means another sleepless night, I took a late afternoon nap. Waking up in the dark is always disorienting, even more so in the evening. I need to hurry to be sure I'm not keeping Grams and making us late for whatever party it is she has us RSVP'd to.

My tux is hanging in the closet in my room at her place. I keep it here, rarely having a need for it outside the city. The stark black pants against the crisp white shirt feel all wrong after weeks of red velvet and white fur trim. I fish a red bow tie out of my top drawer, one with a pocket square to match. Maybe a pop of red will help ease me back into formal society.

A mirror hangs over my dresser, and I take in my reflection. Perfectly put together, with a beard that will become more pepper than salt as the beard coloring fades. My eyes are hollow and bottomless, which isn't the most festive of expressions. I try on a smile and grimace at how forced it looks. Neutral presence that's not a downer is probably going to be the best I can do tonight.

I make my way down the stairs to the main floor of her penthouse apartment, the snow-covered park appearing through the windows as I descend. The waiting figure of disapproval isn't in the foyer like I expect. "Sorry, Grams, didn't mean to hold you up. Is the car outside, or is this the party that sends a horse-drawn carriage to pick up their guests?" My eyes roll as I ask it. Everyone knows you're rich. Is flaunting it really necessary?

No answer, which is strange. Maybe she went into the library for a pre-party drink? I walk past the opulent Christmas decorations lining every surface—garland, holly, and golden ornaments large enough to fall off most tree branches if you tried to hang them.

The door to the office is open, the glow of multicolored lights shining out into the hallway. Grams would never have a tree with colorful lights out in the open. But in her office, she made sure to put up a tree with the ability to display both white and multicolored lights, depending on her mood and whether she's alone.

"I wasn't that late, but if we're having drinks, I'll have . . ." My words trail off as I take in the room around me. My grandma is nowhere to be seen, but instead Santa is standing next to the tree, his back to me, looking out the window.

I pinch my thigh. Am I still dreaming and this is my mind's way of saying I've maybe taken the Santa thing far enough?

Then, Santa turns around, and my heart rises into my throat.

"Austin?" I breathe out, not sure I put enough volume into my voice to carry across the room.

"Hi, Brody," he says, holding his arms out to show off what he's wearing, like I could miss it. "What do you think?"

Even before he asked, my eyes were drinking him in. The few inches and muscle mass he has on me helps him fill out the suit better than I expected. The way his eyes are trained on me, a hopeful light shining within them, and his small smile is what I really notice though. Austin is here.

"How? Why?" I ask, hoping the power of complex sentences comes back soon. I have a lot I want to say, something I very much need to say.

Austin shrugs, all nonchalant, but the way his smile grows reveals just how proud of his plan he is. "I've always heard great things about New York at Christmastime. Thought I might check it out for myself." When I don't say anything, he takes a step closer. Like a magnet, I take one too. "But as for logistics, I called Blaire to get your grandma's address and phone number off your emergency contact form." I bark out a laugh, and he chuckles too.

"Turns out I didn't need to ask her to break her strong code of ethics, because you added a local emergency contact a few weeks ago. Right after your migraine. She felt comfortable sharing those contact details. Since it's an emergency."

My cheeks heat, and not from the warmth of the electric fire crackling in the fireplace. "I probably should have asked, but since you were my roommate at the time—"

Austin crosses the rest of the space between us in an instant. "You were never my roommate. You were always so much more."

I reach out to caress his face, still not believing he's standing in front of me. "But your mom and Christmas? She's okay you're here?"

He laughs again, the joy in the sound untying the knot that's been wedged in my gut since I got on the train. "I'm confident in saying she may not have let me into the house tomorrow if I showed up there instead of coming here. I need to say I'm sorry for pushing you away on the car ride on Sunday. I didn't believe you'd want to keep me around once you got back to your life here. I should have taken a risk."

I tangle my other hand with his, needing to keep him here. In this moment with me. "Every day for the last two weeks, I've wanted to talk about what happens next. But we were in such a good place, I didn't want to ruin it with talks of the future."

"I know it was supposed be just sex, but—"

The rest of his sentence is lost, my lips meeting his, his mouth on mine like coming home. I pull back enough to see his eyes, to make him hear me. "It was never just sex. With you, it's always been everything."

Our lips meet again, and he lets go of my hand to slide his arms around my back and draw me flush to his body.

The kiss slows, and we stand there, breathing each other in.

"I also should have told you on the ride," I say, taking a deep breath and a leap. "I love you. I'm don't think I ever stopped."

His eyes crinkle with the width of his smile. "I love you, too. There's a fine line between love and hate—even when I thought it was the latter, not all of my heart was able to cross that line."

"That may be the most romantic way someone's ever told someone else they hated them," I say, and lean in to take his lips again when my phone beeps in my pocket. As much as I don't want an interruption, I assume it's a message from my grandma.

GRAMS

You were late, so I left without you. I think you'll be happy with the alternative plans for your evening. Breakfast is at 9:00 a.m. sharp. There are pajamas for you both under the tree.

"What'd she say?" Austin asks, his lips trailing over my neck while my attention is on my phone.

"She's out for the evening and expects us both at breakfast in the morning. In matching PJs."

He laughs, his breath tickling my ear before he pulls back so I can see his face. "I think I'm going to like your grams."

"I'm certain she's going to love you, which will cause all sorts of hell for me."

Austin shrugs. "Worth it."

"Absolutely," I say, without a drop of irony.

We stand there, taking in the moment in the glow of my favorite tree in the entire apartment.

"Well, if we have until 9:00 a.m., how will we pass the time?" Austin asks, his voice wicked.

"Oh, I have some ideas," I say, taking his hand and leading him down the hallway. We walk back past the large tree in the living area with the presents underneath it and up the stairs to my room. "And you won't be needing those PJs quite yet."

"Mmm," Austin hums, and I'm grateful Grams gives the staff Christmas Eve and Christmas Day off. "I know I have a thing for the Santa suit, but this tux is really working for me too. What other types of suits can you inspire an obsession with? Bathing suits? Maybe a clown suit?"

Make that very, very grateful.

Soon enough, we're behind the closed door of my room. There're so many ways I want to show this man how much I love him—I'm not quite sure where to start.

He steps forward and envelops me in a hug. Our bodies press together at every matching point we have, and he squeezes me tight. It's a hug full of love and affection, and I can feel his relief at having me in his arms, of being back in mine. And in that instant, I know exactly what I want.

"Austin," I start.

"Hmm?" he hums, the noise content.

"I want you to fuck me."

Chapter 25

Austin

I pull back to look at Brody's face. What I find there is nothing but trust and love, but I have to check.

"Are you sure? Really, it's okay—"

"I'm not saying I never want to top you again, but I'm ready. I want to share this with you." He seals his words with a kiss, his tongue tracing the seam of my lips and asking for more. I open, allowing his tongue to tangle with mine. My hands run up the side of his body, across the front of his shoulders until they find the lapels of his jacket. I push toward the back of his shoulders, letting it fall to the ground.

His hands undo the sash of my jacket and start to repeat the same motion. He pauses when his fingers meet skin and pulls his mouth away. "Are you shirtless under here?" Finishing the job of pushing the jacket off my shoulders, he takes in the sight of me, hat, suspenders and pants. I know it's a good look from checking the mirror earlier, but Brody looks like he wants to devour me.

"Okay, I think I'm beginning to understand your Santa kink," he says, running his fingers over the elastic holding my pants into place. He pulls the suspender back slightly and lets it go, so it snaps against my nipple. I hiss, and he immediately bends, pushing the fabric out of the way so it hangs off my arm, and licks away the sting on my skin with his tongue. The snap on the other side is harder, but I'm ready this time, and the immediate hit of pain turns to pleasure with his warm, wet mouth circling the tight bud.

With the suspenders off my shoulders, the pants fall to the ground. It's a good thing too, because my cock is leaking enough to form a wet spot through my underwear. Shirtless in the Santa suit is one thing, but commando felt a bridge too far. He reads my mind. "I wondered if I'd find you bare under the pants too." His finger slides under the elastic of my boxer briefs with dancing Santa Clauses on them, starting under my belly button and tracing to my ass crack. He brings his finger back to the front, dipping further in to swipe some pre-cum from my slit. My knees come close to buckling at the touch.

"Obviously, it would have been too messy," I say, a growl leaving my chest as I watch him bring the liquid from my cock to his mouth. "You've got too many clothes on." I step so we're chest to chest. "Do you have more of these shirts?" He nods.

"Good," I say, before tucking my hands between the halves and with a ripping motion send several of the buttons flying. The bowtie I forgot to consider holds the shirt together at his neck. "You know," I mutter, all too aware Brody's trying not to laugh at my annoyance. "If I knew how to tie one of these things, I might make you wear this and only this while I fuck you."

"I'll teach you," he says, extending his face up for a kiss. I slide the bowtie from the collar and undo the final button in the appropriate way. Brody holds up his arms, and I take care of the cuff links holding the shirt on his wrists.

"This never happens in the movies." I take the cuff links and set them on the dresser next to us.

"This is better than any movie, because it's us."

"That's a good line," I say, my heart swelling in my chest. "And I'm not at all being sarcastic." My mouth goes to work on his neck while I open his pants. Much like mine before, his pants fall right to the ground. He steps out of them, taking my mouth and the rest of me with him. I pull Brody's body tight against me, moaning at the feeling of his skin against mine. It's only been days since I felt it, and only a few hours where I worried I'd never feel it again. But I hope I never take it for granted. Our tongues tangle as we fight for dominance, until I grip his hair, positioning his mouth how I want it. He allows me to take what I need from his kiss, all too happy to be swept along in my passion.

I realize we're grinding our cocks together, and I will not allow Christmas orgasms to be ones where we finish in our underwear. I untangle myself from Brody and take a step back, admiring my handiwork. His hair askew, his lips swollen and face flushed. I want to take him apart.

"Get yourself ready for me," I say, my voice deep and full of desire. His eyes widen, and his cock jerks underneath the cloth of his boxer briefs, telling me he's into it. He nods.

"On the bed, then." I jerk my chin to indicate where I want him. Stopping at the bedside table, he pulls out a bottle of lube and pushes down his briefs, letting his cock spring free. He climbs on the bed, propping his head on a pillow. I keep myself at the foot and fight to keep my hands at my sides and not on my body.

Brody takes a deep breath and coats his finger in lube. Reaching down between his legs, he circles his hole before pushing the tip of his finger inside. His other hand grasps at his cock and gives it slow, loose strokes. He wipes at the moisture gathering at the tip and uses that to glide up and down. Little by little, he sinks his finger in, until he's working it in and out of himself at a pace matching the strokes of his cock.

"God, what a sight you are, baby. Merry Christmas to me," I say, squeezing hard at the bulge in the front of my underwear. "Tell me, how does it feel?"

"Feels good," he says, his voice strained. "Not as good as your finger though." Brody had asked for a little ass play at points when I sucked his dick, but I never gave him more than one.

"Try adding one more," I say. "Then it might feel better than me." He pulls his hand free to add a bit more lube, and then he's back at his opening, pushing a second finger in.

"Take out your cock," he says, my eyes locked on where his two fingers are disappearing. "I want to see it."

I push my briefs to the ground and grab my cock firmly at the base, not giving in to the urge to stroke. "Like what you see? I know I do."

He nods, another groan as his hand twitches. He must have just added another finger. "I can see you leaking from here."

"I'm dying to put my mouth on you," I say. "How would that feel right now?"

"Please, I need your mouth," he groans. I climb onto the bed and crawl to where he is. The sight of his hole being stretched by three fingers is even better up close. But I don't want to look anymore. I want to touch. I stop the motions of his hand on an out stroke and pull his fingers the rest of the way out and replace them with three of mine. His hips arch and I feel his muscles clench around us.

"You're opening up so good for me," I say, continuing to move my hand in time with his. I lean down and take him in my mouth, bobbing up and down for a few strokes before swirling my tongue around the angry red head. I move down to suck one of his balls in my mouth, our hands bumping against my chin.

"Austin, please, I'm ready," he begs.

"Say it again." Our hands pull completely out of his body this time.

"Please, can I have your cock?" His eyes are open wide, like he might break apart if I don't fill him where he's empty.

"However—whenever you want it."

"I want to ride you," he says, swallowing hard at whatever he's picturing.

I catch up to his vision and scramble up next to his head, pressing a kiss to his lips. He pulls himself into a sitting position and kneels in front of me. Opening the bottle of lube, he pours some in his hand and slicks up my cock. I hiss at the contact, beyond ready to feel him with nothing between us. I just hope I can manage not to blow the moment I'm buried inside him.

Brody moves my hand to the base of my cock, and I hold it up for him as he straddles me. Using my shoulders as support, he lowers himself onto me.

"Nice and slow," I say, knowing from this angle he'll feel extra full.

Brody shakes his head and drops himself in one motion until he's full of my cock. We both groan at the sudden change in sensation.

"You're squeezing me so tight."

"I was made to take your cock. You fill me so good." His eyes open from being squeezed tight and lock with mine. "Ready?"

"Ready," I say, and Brody starts a slow grind on my dick. His movements are small, but they send sparks up my spine. He starts riding me harder, pushing himself up and down my shaft, shifting so he gets the angle just right.

"Oh!" he cries. I grip his hips so we can repeat the motion, lighting him up from the inside. Our movement in the mirror across from the bed catches my eye then, and I watch as Brody moves up and down, taking all of me into his body. Only he and I, with nothing between.

"Baby, I wish you could see how good you look taking me." I nod at the mirror. He twists to look over his shoulder. I see in the mirror his eyes are locked on where I disappear and reappear with his thrusts.

"Fuck," he says, turning back to face me and taking my mouth. He pushes his fingers into my hair, gripping tight as his ass grips me tighter. I reach between us and stroke his cock in time with our thrusts.

"I'm so close," he says, his lips still moving against mine, like he can't bear to lose the contact.

"Let me see you fall," I say, pulling away and watching as Brody's face tightens in ecstasy. His movements falter as he comes, spraying both of our chests with his release. I thrust up into him through his orgasm, trying to extend his pleasure, until the pressure around my cock is too much and I empty into him.

Brody slumps against me, his arms tight around my shoulders. I wrap mine around his back and trace a pattern from the top of his ass to his shoulder blades. Moments pass by as we stay tangled up in each other. He pulls back and pushes the sweaty hair off my forehead.

"I love you," he says, staring into my eyes and it feels like he can see into my soul. He smiles as if he likes what he finds.

"I love you, too." The feelings of hope and contentment filling me up in this moment are unlike anything I've ever felt, even ten years ago. This version of Austin and Brody is stronger and more sure.

"The ensuite has a bathtub big enough for two. And peppermint bubble bath."

I lean forward and place a peck on his lips. "As long as you're there, it sounds like heaven."

The bright light of a new winter's morn wakes me, shining in from between the curtains we forgot to pull closed last night. Brody sucked me off while I sat on the edge of the tub before he snuck downstairs for our pajamas. They didn't quite make it out of the boxes yet, but I'm excited to start new traditions with Brody.

The man in question is plastered against my back and grinding his morning wood against my ass.

"How does Grams handle it if we're late for breakfast?" I ask, my voice froggy with sleep.

"Well, the last time I was late she left you in her place, so I think it might work out for me." His phone vibrates on the side table. "Or it was a one-time thing, and that text is a ten-minute warning." He rolls away from me to check the time and sighs. "Guess it's PJ time, not BJ time."

I laugh, rolling over to face him. "Merry Christmas," I say.

He leans in for a kiss. "Merry Christmas."

We each freshen up in the bathroom and don our white, green, and red plaid, Brody takes my hand and leads me down the stairs, my feet cozy in his back-up slippers.

"Is that my grandson and his beau I hear?" A woman in her 70s wearing a matching set of pajamas appears from the kitchen. "It is! And to think it only took one reminder text."

"Merry Christmas, Grams," Brody says, wrapping one arm around her in a hug while keeping a hold of my hand. "I'd introduce you, but I believe you two have met?"

"Merry Christmas, Mrs. Walker," I say. "Thanks again for the assist last night."

She pulls me into a tight hug, surprisingly strong for a five-foot woman. "Call me Grams. Great to have you here, Austin." Brody's eyes are shining with happiness when we part, taking in the scene in front of him.

"So, what did you boys get up to last night?" We exchange a quick glance, scrambling for something to say. "Never mind. Clearly, I don't want to know. The casserole should be almost done, and I pulled the rolls out right before you came down. Come in and get some coffee."

We sit around the island in the kitchen while Grams tells us all about the party she was at last night and the people she saw. It feels very similar to Christmases at my mom's in a lot of ways, if I can ignore the huge, fancy kitchen and the knowledge there are floor to ceiling windows looking over Central Park in the next room.

"Well," Grams says once we're done and have loaded the dishwasher. "I'm off to take a shower and get ready for our carriage ride. Good thing you're a New England boy and came prepared for the cold, Austin—it's a big park! Then Chinese takeout and Christmas movies in the rec room. Austin, you'll save us from arguing over whose turn it is to pick the third movie this year. My pick is White Christmas and Brody picks—"

"Elf," I finish for her. Grams laughs.

"Our boy does love that goofy tights-and-tunic wearing guy. See you soon, gentlemen." Without another word, she's off.

I lean over the counter, next to where Brody's leaning against his back. "Was it the elf costume that really brought you back to me? Be honest."

He bends down to kiss me. "It didn't hurt."

I shove him lightly, and we both laugh.

"I have something for you. I snuck it under the tree last night when I grabbed our PJs," Brody says, leading the way into the living room.

"Grams had me put my box under there when I got here yesterday. She's serious about Christmas. You know, I expected with all this." I gesture around at the high-end furniture and fixtures around us. "Christmas might be a bit different around here."

"Now you know where I get my spirit," Brody answers. "Before my grandpa died, I think it used to be. But now, she really tries to put people before things or status. We just do it surrounded by all"—he gestures his hands the same way I did—"this."

I nod, soaking it all in. We settle in front of the tree on the carpet, a package in our laps. "Me first," I say. "I think I love giving gifts even more than I love getting them. I didn't have a ton of time. Usually I'm brainstorming the perfect gifts from July, but . . ."

"I'll love it. Because it's from you," Brody says, his eyes alight with happiness. He rips into the paper and opens the box, laughing once he spots what's inside. "My very own Christmas underwear," he says, holding up a striped pair matching the ones I had on his first day in Holly Ridge.

"A vendor sells them at the Christmas market. You have to ask for 'the tinsel' when it's daylight, but they're a big seller."

"Well, thank you. I love them." His fingers worry at the envelope in his lap. "I went a bit of a different route."

"Is it tickets for that vacation in February?" I ask, sliding my finger under the flap and ripping it open.

"Not quite." His bottom lip tucks between his teeth. I unfold the paper inside and stare at the photo, confused.

"This is my mom's house." I keep looking. "This is a listing for my mom's house." I glance up at him, and his face is a picture of trepidation. "The listing says sold. This listing says sold, in my name."

"You kept talking about it being the last Christmas in that house. I know your mom needed to sell it to help pay for the place in Florida."

"You bought my mom's house?" I repeat, dumbfounded. What a silly, romantic man, with apparently more money than sense, I've fallen in love with.

He takes my hand. "Is that okay?"

"I mean, I'm glad I went first with the underwear and all." He laughs, but his eyes are still worried. "I guess I'm just surprised. You bought it not knowing if we. . ."

He nods. "I'm expecting to hear about it from my financial planner after the holidays. But it felt like the perfect gift, especially when Blaire didn't try to talk me out of it. Though, I have to admit, it's a little self-serving."

"How so?" I ask, scooting so I'm sitting next to him. Brody wraps his arm around me and pulls me to his side.

"Well, if I were to need to be in the area for any extended periods of time, I hope you'd let me stay. Even if it's a bit cold for my tastes, Winterberry Glen is my ideal type of town."

I tilt my head so it rests on his shoulder, a smile so wide my cheeks might crack.

"And of course," he continues, "I'd return the favor, letting you stay with me in Stamford anytime you wanted to. I really do think it could check all the boxes of your perfect place to live." He rests his cheek against the top of my head.

"We're going to figure this out, aren't we?" I ask softly, staring at the lights twinkling on the tree. I'm so full of love I could burst.

"As long as you're mine, I don't care where we live."

We sit there for a long time, letting our love and the possibilities for our future surround us. The year may be ending, but our story is just beginning.

Epilogue

One Year Later

Austin

The bed moves at 5:00 a.m. and I groan. "The alarm isn't set to go off for another hour."

"I know, but I can't sleep anymore." The giddiness in my fiancé's voice makes me smile, even if the sun won't rise for almost two more hours.

"So, the morning after Thanksgiving is to a professional Santa what Christmas morning is to kids?" I crack an eye open and watch Brody make sure the lines on his beard are sharp, trimming any stray hairs in the ensuite we remodeled in my mom's house. Something about making her old room our room gave me the willies, so we knocked down a few walls, and built a second master suite on the second floor.

"A very astute observation, fiancé," he says, leaning close to the mirror to examine his work. Since I accepted his proposal last night at dinner, he's referred to me as fiancé about twenty times. It's fucking adorable. "Plus, we've got that special visit to get there early for."

I am excited about the private Santa session we have booked before we open to the public today. The thought gets my feet on the floor and into my slippers. A dull headache from the Thanksgiving turned engagement celebration wine last night beats in my head. A hot shower and caffeine should fix me right up.

"Hi you," I say, wrapping my arms around his middle and pressing a kiss above his ear. I look at us in the mirror and my heart stutters with happiness. How different my life is from a year ago.

"Morning fiancé," he replies, lacing his fingers with mine and leaning against me. "Head feeling okay this morning?" Brody may or may not have warned me against the last two glasses of wine. His hangover rule only applies to Santa—my two-day stint last year will be my only time wearing the beard. I am reprising my role as elf for today only, though, so he may have had a point.

"I'll be all right." I give the side of his head one more kiss before stepping back and turning to the shower. I push down the pumpkin pie boxer briefs Brody presented me with yesterday and turn on the water, waiting for it to warm up.

"When are you going to upgrade me from fiancé to husband?" My question is met with silence. I turn my head and find Brody staring at my ass. I smirk. "You coming or what?" He pushes down his flannel pants and steps up behind me, his cock going into the crease of my ass. "If I have any say, we'll both be coming very soon."

After a longer shower than strictly necessary, we've eaten up all the extra time Brody's early wake-up bought us. By 7:30 a.m., we're out the door, to-go coffee cups in hand. "Susie's going to be offended when we don't stop in this morning," I say, climbing in the passenger seat.

"You can run over this morning sometime and tell her we were running late."

"Should I tell her my future husband was employing his tried-and-true orgasm-headache-recovery method, and we ran out of time?"

"I think we should do a destination wedding in February." Brody ignores my teasing and answers my question from this morning instead. An effective method of shutting me up. "Something small—Grams, your mom, Cole and Blaire, and the girls? I'd marry you anywhere, anytime, but something about picturing you on the beach, looking handsome at sunset, makes my heart swell."

I lace my fingers through his hand resting on my knee and bring it to my mouth for a kiss. "Sounds perfect."

Brody nods. "Can't wait to call you my husband." My heart does that stutter thing again, and if it weren't for the past year of swoonworthy moments like this one, I'd be much more concerned.

We get changed at the high school and walk over to Santa's Workshop. Our special visitors are already inside.

"Cassidy, please don't eat the snow."

"Melody, that's not a present for unwrapping."

Cole and Blaire each scoop up a twin as we round the false wall from the back door. They look a little harried already this morning, but the first day of a holiday festival and managing two sixteen-month-olds will do that.

"Wody!" Cassidy reaches from Blaire's arms for Brody, not at all fooled by his whiter beard and red suit. Blaire and I exchange a look as she hands over her daughter. We're doing this before we open in part because Blaire wanted to be here for their first meeting with Santa, but also because we were worried about this exact thing happening. The girls love their Uncle Brody.

"Pay up," I say to Cole, taking Melody from him as she reaches for me. He pulls out his wallet to hand me a twenty when I realize these tights don't have any pockets. "Later," he says, and turns to watch Cassidy on Brody's lap. The photographer snaps pictures of the two of them and I turn my attention to the little girl in my arms. She looks suspicious of the guy in the red suit.

"Hey now, little butterfly," and her mouth turns up at the special nickname I have for her. "You don't have to be scared. It's Uncle Santa Brody under there. Want to take a closer look?"

She nods before burying her face in my neck. I laugh as I walk over to Brody's chair. Cole pulls Cassidy off his lap to make room for her sister.

"Want to sit on Santa's lap?" I ask. She turns her head so she has one eye open to look at Brody but doesn't seem too sure. "Here, I'll come with you." I sit on Brody's lap, holding Melody in mine. She peers a little closer at him and seems to decide it is Uncle Brody under there, pushing me away and climbing onto his other knee.

"Well, I know when I'm not needed," I joke, and step back to stand next to Blaire and Cole.

"Ready to hang up your elf suit?" Blaire asks. After today, I will be shadowing her and helping as she runs the festival. We're considering starting to host some of our own events, staffed by Brody's Santas, so thought this would be an opportunity to learn from the best. I haven't decided if working for Brody's company is a long-term thing, but I'm happy helping people and getting to work with my partner every day. For now, it's a fit and does, in fact, pay for my health insurance.

"I'll miss the tights, but I know I can always pull them back out if I need to." She shoves me, and I laugh. "What? I meant if I ever need to fill in again. Oh, did you think I meant an s-e-x thing? Mind in the gutter. No wonder you're carrying my nephew." Blaire and Cole found out last week they're having a boy.

She rests her hand on her stomach, just starting to show. Cole takes Cassidy over to sit on Brody's other knee, and the photographer gets photos of both girls together with Santa. "You're getting married before I have this one, right?"

I nod. "I think February. We'll get you the details soon."

She fist pumps. "Cole owes me another twenty. Cleaning him out today."

Blaire steps up to join in for some photos, and Cole slides over. "What do you think—will this be your kids in a year or two?" I imagine it, a photo of Santa and elf dads and some smiling kids. I can see it, but I'm not sure it feels right.

"Maybe." I shrug. "We'd raise the hell out of some awesome

kids. But we also have some awesome nieces and a nephew to spoil rotten. Who knows?"

He squeezes my arm and steps up to join in for some pictures. I look at most of my favorite people, all standing together in one frame. Cole and I finding our people, and those people liking each other? I know I'm lucky.

"Austin." Blaire says my name to get my attention and waves me into the frame. Cole slides over to wrap his arm around Blaire, and I go stand on Brody's other side. He's got a firm grip on each twin to stop them from squirming away, so I wrap my arm around his shoulder and lean in.

As we're smiling, I'm already planning exactly where this photo will go in both the Winterberry Glen and Stamford houses. I want everyone who comes over to see what I'm most proud of in my life—my family.

Acknowledgments

No author is an island and no book gets finished alone. I'm so grateful to everyone who comes along on this journey with me.

Thank you to all my family and friends who put up with canceled plans, grumpy moods, or scattered responses while I pushed to get Brody and Austin's story finished. A special thank you to Kelly, Steph, and Allie for their support and check-ins along the way. And a special shoutout to my Hilton Friends and Family benefactor—those hours spent in Spark by Hilton got this book done.

Thank you Derek for being my MM sensitivity reader. Rachel, thank you for all the voice memos, cheerleading, and always wanting to know how writing's going—so glad we published books on the same day last year. Thank you to Lacey and Cassie for making sure this book makes sense and to Brooke for putting up with my back and forths over the cover art. Thank you everyone who read an ARC, shared a post or reel, and signed up for a PR box. You all make such a difference in an indie author's life. We can't stress that enough.

And to you dear reader—whether you've been with my since we went to Holly Ridge the first time in 2022, started with a Brandt Brother, or are jumping into Brody and Austin for your first story with me: without people to read my words, I'd just be someone talking to their imaginary friends all day.

About the Author

Rachel grew up in Western PA and found her love of reading early in life, supported by her parents with frequent trips to the library and local bookstores. She stumbled into the bookish community in late 2020 and has embraced the bookish lifestyle whole-heartedly, first by diving headfirst into the Romance genre and becoming a book reviewer and Bookstagrammer. In 2021, she changed careers, taking a job at an indie bookstore and starting her first official novel-length writing project.

Rachel has an MFA in Writing Popular Fiction from Seton Hill University, which allowed her to read and write Romance novels for a grade, and is always juggling too many story ideas for one brain to handle. She's excited to continue to write books with heat, heart, and Happily Ever Afters.

Rachel's current Romance series include The Brandt Brothers, a series of interconnected standalones following five brothers set in Washington DC and The Holly Ridge Series, books set in a Christmas-loving small town.

When not immersed in her bookish world, you can find Rachel hanging out with her husband and two cats, spending time with friends in the Washington DC area, and rooting for Pittsburgh sports teams.

Also by Rachel Holm

<u>Holly Ridge Series</u>

Carry Me Through Christmas

Make You Mine This Christmas

<u>The Brandt Brothers Series</u>

Capitally Matched

Capitally Engaged

Capitally Unexpected

Coming Soon: Capitally Yours